The Escape

By Warren Court

The Berlin Escape

Copyright © 2021 Warren Court
All rights reserved.

The characters and events in this book are fictitious. Any similarity to real persons, living or dead, is coincidental and not intended by the author.

For Tina and Katherine

1

September 1934

Rain pelted the fuselage of the RWD-9 in a steady beat. The Polish airplane bucked with the wind, its small wiper worked overtime to clear the deluge from the windscreen. Then, suddenly, the handsome four-seater plane was through the storm and the moon and stars were visible once more. The river shone like a silver ribbon below. Lights from farmhouses and quaint villages dotted its banks.

The plane turned away from the river and headed north, over farmland and vineyards, until the rise of two hills appeared in the distance, exactly where the pilot was told they would be. A dark, flat field surrounded by tall pine trees on all sides appeared in the distance. As the plane approached, signal lights laid out in the shape of an inverted L became visible.

The pilot eased the nose of the high-wing, strut-mounted plane down and reduced the throttle. Slowly the ground rose up to greet it. The signal lights, smudge pots of burning fuel, grew brighter and closer. The pilot squinted at the approaching grassy airstrip, hoping it was just grass, clear of potholes and rocks.

There was the bump of the forward fixed wheels as they hit the ground, a slight rise and then another bump. The pilot eased the throttle back further to bring the aircraft fully down. The plane rushed towards the wall of pine trees at the far end of the field. The pilot ran the length of the field, slowing before reaching the edge of the forest and then spinning the tail around for a takeoff.

Aubrey Endeavours removed her leather flying cap and shook her curly auburn hair loose. She looked longingly at the thermos of coffee and yawned. There wouldn't even be time for a sip. She would have to wait until she was safely on the ground again in Belgium.

The plane's motor throbbed in perfect pitch and she checked her fuel levels. Half a tank left; plenty to get her across the border. She was well chuffed with this little airplane. Unfamiliar with it when she'd taken off from Mokotowskie Airfield, Warsaw, twelve hours earlier, she was now very comfortable. She and the machine were becoming fast friends.

Aubrey was competing in the air-rally portion of the Challenge International de Tourisme. Since 1929, Poland, France, Germany, Czechoslovakia and other European countries started meeting to compete and to showcase planes capable of carrying two or more passengers, the intent being the advancement of commercial air travel. There were several phases to the competition: short runway takeoffs and landings, fuel consumption trials, and the final competition, a grand rally around Europe and North Africa.

This year's host nation, Poland, was the start and finishing line for the rally that saw nineteen flyers touching down in Germany, Belgium, France and Spain, then going on to Casablanca and across the desert to Tunis. From there the racers headed north to Sicily and the Italian boot before weaving their way up the Balkans to arrive back in Poland. It was a ninety-five-hundred-mile endurance race that pushed men, and one woman, and their machines to the edge.

This was not Aubrey's first air rally; she was a seasoned aviatrix from America. She'd flown her Sopwith Camel biplane in countless rallies and races and performed stunts from coast to coast.

But her flying career had been cut short when a sudden vortex of wind had forced her down into a farmer's field in Ohio two years ago. Aubrey had spent six weeks in hospital with a fractured pelvis, a broken arm and concussion. Her beloved Sopwith had suffered even more; it was totalled and sold for scrap. And without the funds to purchase another plane, she was grounded.

Then this opportunity to participate in the European air rally had fallen into her lap. At last, a chance to get behind the stick again. She'd leapt at it.

But there were strings. A return to air racing and, potentially, a whiff of her former fame and winnings were not the real purpose. No, she was putting the borrowed Polish plane down in this field in western Germany for an entirely different reason.

Aubrey scanned the surrounding forest and then checked her watch. He had to be out there; who else would set the smudge pots ablaze? Their flickering flames were already dying down. Then she saw him break cover, dressed in a dark jacket and pants with a tan cap on his head. He came running at the airplane head on, straight at the propellor.

"No!" Aubrey screamed, as she saw what was about to happen. She'd seen propellor strikes before; they were horrific. Traumatizing to the witnesses, brutally fatal to the victims. The man pulled up short of the spinning propellor and ran around the tail end of the airplane. The RWD-9, a four-seater passenger plane, had two sets of doors. The man got into the rear passenger seat.

Aubrey didn't look at him. She was concerned with several sets of moving lights that were rippling through the trees to one side of them: vehicles were descending on the area. Given the clandestine nature of the pickup, she could only surmise they were bad news. When she heard the rear passenger door slam shut, she pushed the throttle forward and the plane started bounding down the makeshift runway.

Amidst the blur of trees passing by, she could see silhouettes of men moving towards her. She saw flashes, presumably from guns, but heard no shots over the sound of the RWD's engine. Then the glass on one of the side windows was punctured and a bullet whizzed through the cockpit, narrowly missing her. Aubrey didn't have time to react. The band of forest in front of her was rapidly approaching. The plane reached takeoff speed and seemed to want to go airborne all on its own. Aubrey had to pull the yoke back ever so slightly to allow the plane to leap upwards into the air. The tandem set of controls in the empty seat next to her moved as well, as if some invisible pilot was helping.

The forest passed beneath her and she breathed a sigh of relief. A quick course change to point them straight at the Belgian frontier, and then she could relax. The vacant field and the men shooting at her were left behind them as they climbed higher, passing through a bank of clouds. Then suddenly they were floating on a carpet of fluffy white cotton with the moon above to light the way. All was good in the world.

The wind whistled in through the bullet hole in the cockpit. She felt bad about that. This plane wasn't hers. It was a loaner from the manufacturer in Warsaw. She was familiar with these European air rallies, but had never dreamed of flying in one. American airplane manufacturers had toyed with the idea of entering a team, but it had never progressed beyond whimsical ideation. And besides, if they did put a team together, it would inevitably be an all-male team.

The age of the sensational female aviatrix was quickly coming to a close. Aubrey could see the writing on the wall. The barnstormers and wing walkers had long since vanished. There were no more records to achieve; Lindbergh had conquered the Atlantic. Amelia Earhart, an acquaintance of Aubrey's, had done the same thing as the first female. Now, the far reaches of the continents had been reached by airplane, and the age of commercial air travel was upon them. Her beloved father had quipped that, eventually, a pilot would have no more prominence in society than a bus driver. And there weren't a lot of female bus drivers around. And if there were, no one noticed them.

She thought of him now, back on the family farm in Michigan, dealing with demons he'd brought home from the Great War. A heroic flyer in his own right, he'd returned a decorated but defeated man, the spark in his eye gone, his ambition and drive sapped by horrors experienced on the Western Front where he commanded a squadron of French-built SPAD fighters.

But he would be proud of her now, although he wouldn't admit it, of course. Instead, he'd give her a verbal hide-tanning for being foolish enough to get hooked up in this crazy scheme to pluck a stranger out of Nazi Germany. But secretly, he would be proud of her bravery and skill.

She speculated who it was exactly she had tucked into the seat behind her. Was he a spy, a man on the run? This had all come about so quickly. One moment she was sitting in her father's study in Michigan; the next, she'd been on a steamer bound for Europe. She'd landed in Danzig and was delivered to Warsaw with some of her former celebrity reinvigorated. The Poles had been gracious; they celebrated strong women. The German participants seemed aloof, except for one pilot named Albert whom she'd briefly talked to. He'd shown her a picture of his infant son and wife.

She had at first been anxious about the presence of Germans. She'd expected the jackboots, skull and crossbones of the SS. But these men were flyers, first and foremost. They wore the blue uniform of the newly formed Luftwaffe, Hitler's air force.

Their planes looked fast. The Bf 109s were sleeker and more modern-looking than the other planes. But she did eventually see swastikas painted on them. That hideous design sent shivers down her spine. Like most Americans, she'd watched the newsreels in movie theatres. Most of those newsreels showed sporting events or beauty pageants, and the crowds soaked them up. Occasionally, though, they gave viewers a glimpse of what was going on in the world and who was shaping events. Like that demonic-looking man with the strange moustache who seemed to have a whole nation entranced. She'd read about the rising tensions in Europe, the ambitious leader of the Third Reich and his thoughts on racial purity. She'd read of the ever-increasing rules, harsh laws that were further marginalizing and isolating the minority population in Germany.

When she encountered these sons of the Reich on that Polish airfield, she was tempted to share her thoughts on the matter. But she remembered what she was there to do, how important it was. And her job wasn't to win any air race. No, her real mission, now halfway complete, was of far greater importance.

Now that the plane was levelled out and heading in the right direction, she could glance back at him. He was shrouded in the dark confines of the tiny cockpit, his arms across his chest, his head lowered. A slight gurgling sound came from him; the man was fast asleep. She was astounded; they'd just been shot at. Maybe he'd been waiting in the forest a long time and was exhausted. He was now safely tucked away in the airplane, with a competent pilot at the controls. Should she take his slumber as a compliment?

But who was he? *Aubrey, face it*, she thought. *You'll probably never know*. The man who had arranged the whole thing was a complete mystery to her. Why should this "package," as he'd described the human being she'd just rescued from the clutches of the Nazis, be any less of an enigma?

But at least she knew the identity of that first mystery man: it was her uncle, Arthur Colins.

There was a slight bump of turbulence, enough to wake her passenger.

"Coffee here if you want it," she called back to him. He gave a grunt of a reply, and a withered hand reached between the forward seats to retrieve the thermos.

"*Danke.*"

"Good thing we got out of there when we did. They were shooting at us."

"Yes, a good thing," the man replied.

"Who were they?"

She heard the man slurp some coffee and then the thermos was returned.

"I said, who were those guys with guns—Nazis?"

No reply.

Aubrey was more than a little perturbed. After all, it was her neck on the line. That bullet could easily have hit her. There had never been any mention of guys with guns. The adrenaline rush of the clandestine landing and hurried takeoff under fire was waning, and now she had time to reflect. What was it all for? She'd asked Uncle Arthur for some details, but he had politely but firmly told her that she had no need to know.

When her uncle had first come to her with his proposition, she'd hardly been able to believe it. She would be entered into the rally, a guest of the Polish government. The Poles knew of her exploits. She would be given a plane to fly. But any offer of a mechanic to fly with her, which was standard, should be politely refused, Arthur told her. She would fly alone.

The two of them had sent her father to bed and then pored over a map of western Germany. Landmarks were identified, instructions given. Arthur had made her repeat them over and over: Fly west from Bonn for two hours up the Rhine River. At the Edelweiss Bridge follow the eastern tributary for another hour. Find the town with the Gothic dome in the centre and then turn northward. Look for the two hills like giant burial mounds in the distance: she couldn't miss them. The field would be right in front of her.

He'd explained the signal lights and how they were arranged: three lights in an inverted L if everything was fine. Three lights in a straight line if all was not well. Somebody might have a gun to the man's head. Aubrey asked why? What had he done? Her uncle did not answer.

None of the material Arthur had shown her could travel with her. He didn't have to tell her why; this was spy stuff. It confirmed for her that Uncle Arthur was involved in espionage. Her father, in one of his lighter drinking moments, before the screaming night terrors, had mentioned that Arthur worked for G2, Army Intelligence, during the war. And that he'd never really left it after the Armistice.

The drone of the aircraft and twelve hours of flying began to take its toll. Aubrey had forgotten what it was like to fly long distances alone. No one to engage in conversation to keep the senses alert. She looked down at the thermos. Why not? She needed fuel as well. With one hand she spun the cap off the thermos and put it between her thighs. There was a bit more turbulence than in a flat spot of smooth flying. She poured some coffee.

The thudding sound of machine guns and the lines of tracer that tore into the aircraft jolted her from the task, and hot coffee spilled onto her thighs. She winced as the fighters that had just shot at her flew by. They dove in front of her, banked to the left and started to rise.

Aubrey threw the thermos into the footwell of the cockpit, cranked the yoke to the right and dove. The whistling sound from the punctured fuselage was louder now, and she found the controls slightly sluggish. A quick glance to the right and she saw a stitch-line of bullet holes in the cockpit.

She whipped her head around crazily, looking for the two fighters. She had seen ones like them when she'd refuelled at Tempelhof Airport outside of Berlin. Heinkel 51s, the latest fighter planes of the Third Reich. Menacingly efficient biplanes with large, narrow bodies and Art Deco styling. The top wings pressed tight over the cockpit. The muzzles of twin machine guns visible. They had looked like hawks on that runway, waiting to take off after prey.

And now the hawks were here, and she was the prey.

Aubrey pushed the yoke forward and banked over to the left. She dove for the clouds; the pillowy blanket rushed up at her. There was more firing; the Heinkels had speed and obvious firepower, but her civilian plane had agility. This was one contest she was not prepared for, but it was the one contest she had to win.

Aubrey spiralled the aircraft downwards and was engulfed in whiteness. The windscreen was slick with water in an instant. She heard the man behind her gasp once. She pulled back on the yoke just as she punched through the bottom of the clouds. The German countryside was rushing up at her. Or was it already Belgian dirt she was about to embrace? The thoughts of crashing again were planted firmly in her mind. She summoned superhuman strength to regain control of the aircraft and pulled it back up level, just two hundred feet from the ground. She looked around wildly, but the confines of the enclosed cockpit robbed her of vision. Where were the Heinkels?

Aubrey brought the plane closer to the ground and heard the passenger shout something in German. She had no time discuss her tactics with him. She was going to suck the contours of the land and try to vanish in them. The plane was painted a dark blue on top, and she hoped it would help her blend in.

No such luck: her plane shuddered as the heavy rounds impacted its skin, and she heard something snap and pop on her starboard side. The engine shuddered, and she pulled the yoke back to gain height. She barrel-rolled and swung around in a one-eighty, and then saw the second plane coming at her. He'd overshot, and tracer rounds reached out, searching for her. They went harmlessly past and kicked up soil in a farmer's field.

Aubrey kept the plane in a tight turn, scrambling for altitude while avoiding stall speed. The engine groaned and sputtered under this manoeuvre and she was forced to level off to regain speed. She spotted the two black shapes of the Heinkels out in front of her and turned towards them. They were circling too, trying to spin around and line up another pass. Another good one like they'd just had and she was done for.

The distance closed. The planes were still in their turn to the left, one in front of the other. Probably the most experienced pilot was leading the second. Or maybe the master was letting a newbie get his first kill? Aubrey moved into their slipstream and positioned herself behind the rear of the second fighter. If she'd only had guns herself, she could fire at them. Maybe just scare them off. Or, if necessary, send them hurtling to the ground in a fiery wreck. But she had no guns, just her intuition and two thousand hours of flying time.

The tables were turned and now her positioning robbed her hunters of their vision. They could not see her. She closed the distance; her plane was just a tad more manoeuvrable. She toyed with the idea of flying up beside the rear plane and flipping the pilot the bird.

Around and around they went, gaining altitude, then losing it as the German fighters searched for her. She had plenty of fuel, but what about them? If the German authorities were on to the man in the rear of her plane, they would have had to have these fighters already airborne when she'd landed to pick him up. They'd been up there, waiting for her to take off if she got away from the guys on the ground. And gotten away she had. She knew fighters were like sports cars: great fun to ride in but hell on fuel economy.

After a dizzying two minutes of her trailing them, the lead fighter banked hard to the right and swooped down. The other one seemed reluctant to do so at first, but then followed suit. She flew above them. Unless they had eyes in the backs of their heads, she was still invisible to them. They were heading east, back into German territory, convinced they'd lost her. She was giddy with joy; her ploy had worked. The fighters increased their speed and left her. She then turned back westward and rose slowly up into the cloud cover and onwards to Belgium.

2

The sun was rising behind her by the time she crossed the border. She had the map of north-eastern Belgium resting on her thigh. The plane had suffered damage but was still airworthy. The cockpit had been punctured by machine gun bullets, and the controls were stiff. A control cable to one of the ailerons must have been shot to bits. She should by all rights put the aircraft down; there could be more cables or wooden spars on the verge of giving out, she knew. But she wanted to complete the mission. The rendezvous spot was twenty miles over the border. Thankfully, the sun was dissipating the morning fog and she could make out landmarks of the Belgian countryside.

She realized that this terrain would be similar to what her father had flown over seventeen years before, during the Great War. There were Flemish windmills, and smoke rising from chimneys. She had dead reckoned fairly accurately and saw the rendezvous spot approaching in the distance.

Her passenger was silent, and she didn't have time to try to speak to him. *Just get the airplane down, hand him over to the friendlies and be on your way.* There was a proper airport nearby; she could put down there after dropping the man off and see to getting the damage to her plane repaired. With any luck, she might be able to continue on in the rally. She might even make up the time and place fairly well. If she managed to get in the top ten, it might even make the newspapers back home. She had visions of her career being revived, and for a few minutes she smiled to herself at the prospect of being on top again. She might gain a sponsor, one who would put her behind the controls of another plane. One she could call all her own.

She wouldn't mind owning one of these Polish planes, if any were being exported. She definitely wanted an upgraded aircraft; the era of the biplane was at an end. Then she remembered the deadly effectiveness of the two Heinkel fighters she'd encountered and thought better of it.

She saw the town of Dinant, its distinctive cathedral and Belgian flag a welcome indicator of her location. She checked her Longines wristwatch, given to her by a close friend just before he died. She was on time. Even after that dalliance with the German fighters she'd managed to stay on schedule.

Outside of the town, she found the country road. It was long and flat and deserted. Ideal. There were grassy fields on either side where she could pull off. She suspected that, after dropping her passenger off and doing a quick inspection, she could be on the way to that nearby airport in a matter of minutes. This touch-down and takeoff was going to go a lot easier than the one in Germany, no doubt.

She throttled back, flared and came in for a perfect low, single-bounce landing on the dirt road. She brought the aircraft to a slow crawl and manoeuvred off the road into the nearest field. It was only after the engine was shut off that she heard moaning from the rear of the cockpit. She turned to look and recoiled in horror. Her passenger was slumped back in the seat, his clothes drenched in blood. The skin on his face looked waxy.

Aubrey quickly climbed back and unbuckled him, and another gush of blood came out of his stomach. She saw a large tear in the stretched aluminum where a round from the fighters had punctured it and torn into the man.

He moaned again. It took all her strength to get him out of the rear seat and over the lip of the rear doors. She dropped down to the ground and pulled him down after her, grunting as she took his weight. Blood splattered onto the Belgian field as she dragged him away from the aircraft and laid him down. She took her leather flying jacket off, rolled it up and put it under his head. He smiled up at her.

"Am I free?"

"You're in Belgium."

He smiled again, then started to cry.

"Hang in there," she told him. "Help is on the way."

"I'm dead. But I'm free. Listen to me, girl." The man spoke in a German accent. "You must listen to me about Lazarus. He must be set free. They have him."

She tried to calm him. He tried to prop himself up on his elbows to let her know he was serious, but he collapsed back in pain. The ground beneath him was saturated with blood.

"Lazarus, they have him. Here." He took a photo out of his pocket. "Write to Lydia. Tell her I died a free man." He thrust a photo at her. She didn't even look at it; she just held his hand, crumpling the photo.

"Tell her."

"You're going to be okay." She heard a vehicle approaching. "You're going to be okay."

"Tell Lydia I died a free man. Tell her I'm sorry." The man didn't finish the last word. His mouth was frozen open and he died looking into a stranger's eyes.

Aubrey wiped a way a tear away as the truck came roaring down the road. She watched it approach. The photo went into her pants pocket and she stood as the men got out of the truck.

There were three of them. Two seemed to be workmen, and they ran to the aircraft. The other was more casual, dressed in a suit and tie with an overcoat. He walked over to Aubrey.

"He's dead," she said.

"I can see that," he said.

"Who is he?"

"None of your concern. He's nobody now. Pascal!" the man called, and the two men came over to the dead agent and picked him up by his arms and legs. They carried him to the back of the truck.

"Are you alright?" the man asked. He had a distinct upper-class British accent, and he retrieved a silver cigarette case from his coat pocket. He offered one to Aubrey. She shook her head.

"I want to get out of here. There's an airport near here. They can repair the plane and I can continue the rally."

The man stood smoking a cigarette and looked the plane over. "Not sure it's worth it."

The two men came back, carrying jerry cans. Aubrey thought they were going to refuel the Polish plane. Awfully nice of them.

"What happened?"

"We were ambushed. He got on board and the whole place lit up with fireworks. Gunfire," she said. "We took off. I almost got my butt shot off in the process. Then we were attacked by German fighters. Two of them. Heinkel 51s, I think. They nearly got us." She realized how foolish her words were, given one of them was lying dead in the back of a truck.

"But you managed to outmanoeuvre them?"

"I did. Got right in behind them. They thought they lost me."

The man smiled and nodded as he puffed on his cigarette. "We should get going."

"Yes. I'm heading south."

"Really?" the man said. Aubrey heard splashing, and realized the men were dousing the plane in gasoline. She started to run towards them. The man with the cigarette grabbed her arm and held her. He was strong and pulled her back.

"What are you doing? That's my plane!"

"No, it's not. Pascal, if you please." One of the Belgians took the two jerry cans back to the truck. The man named Pascal had a stick with a rag tied to it, and he set fire to it. He approached the plane and touched its nose, which was glistening with gasoline. The whole thing went up in a *whoosh*. They were pushed back by the flames.

"Get in the truck, before the petrol tank goes." The Englishman pulled on her arm and they began to run. They got halfway to the vehicle when the plane's fuel tanks ignited with a roar. The exquisite Polish airplane was strewn all over the field.

Aubrey kept silent until she was in the back of the truck with the British man and the dead agent. At least they'd put a blanket over him. The other two fellows got in the front.

"You crashed," the British man said as she opened her mouth to speak. "You entered the rally and made it across Germany, but bad weather forced you down in this field. You survived, miraculously unscathed."

"And him?"

"Never mind about him. He was never here. *We* were never here. Is that understood?"

"What about Lazarus?"

"I don't know who that is. Did he say something?"

"I think that's what he said," she lied. "He died just after."

"We're going to let you out near the town. You'll walk the rest of the way. You'll tell them you crashed. They'll come back out with you to the field. Afterwards, you can make contact with your embassy."

"Guess I'm out of the race."

"You were never really in it."

Aubrey kept her eyes on the retreating countryside for the rest of the drive.

3

The Sopwith Camel's stick bucked and jarred so much so that Aubrey had to grip it tightly with both hands. The thick leather gloves she wore not only kept her hands warm but provided grip on the polished piece of maple and reduced vibration. She'd never flown in weather like this before. She'd been delayed on the ground for over an hour because of engine trouble; the other competitors in the race across the Rocky Mountains had left on time and the judges had been on the verge of disqualifying her when her mechanic finally got the 130-horsepower engine going with a roar. If they had actually disqualified her, she didn't know it. Nor had she cared. Aubrey had roared down the runway past the judges stand and was airborne. That takeoff had been in blue skies without a cloud in sight.

But as she approached the Gillette Pass west of the Black Hills of South Dakota, the sky turned a violent purple. She could see lightning strikes hitting the ground. She scanned ahead for a suitable place to land. Maybe the storm would pass quickly and she could get back up and finish this race. Coming in dead last was not what she was hoping for. But coming in just plain dead looked like a very real possibility if she kept going.

This was a timed trial; the flyer with the quickest passage across the continental divide would win the prize—two thousand dollars and a brand-new Model A Ford roadster. It didn't matter that she was an hour late in taking off. All that mattered was how quickly she flew. But a ten- or fifteen-minute wait on the ground while the storm passed would almost certainly rob her of placing even a respectable third.

Aubrey couldn't think about that now; the wind was throwing her plane wildly around the sky. It was a struggle just to keep airborne. She had to get down, and fast. There was a winding road down there, no more than a dirt-covered track with barbed wire fences on either side.

The road straightened out for a mile ahead of her and rose on a hill. That would help bring her to a stop quicker. She decided to go for it. Then, as if Mother Nature had heard her plea, the storm ceased its onslaught and her plane levelled out. She flew along over the road just in case. Now she could see a patch of blue in amongst the dark thunderheads and sunlight poured through it, cascading across a field of hay. Cows huddled together in the distance.

She had a choice to make: land and wait the storm out, or carry on. While she weighed the decision, the hand of God, in the form of wind shear, pushed down on her plane with tremendous force. The tendons in her arms straining, her back screaming in agony, Aubrey pulled on the stick to save her plane, save herself. All to no avail. She slammed into the earth at close to a hundred miles an hour.

Aubrey woke with a start, sat straight up in bed and clutched her chest. She looked around and remembered where she was: in her bed in her childhood home in Michigan.

There was a phlegm-choked snore and a cough from the room down the hall where her father slept. She sighed and collapsed back onto the bed. The nightmare of the crash faded away. It had been months since she'd last had it. She'd almost forgotten what it was like.

She rolled over on her side and looked at her dresser. The moonlight lit up the framed black and white photographs. One was of her when she was five. Another at twelve with a horse. Then one of her in the cockpit of a plane, the first time she'd gone for a flight at the local fair. The barnstormer had taken her up, circled over town. She'd begged him to do a barrel roll or loop-the-loop. He'd obliged the thrill-seeking girl with a quick dive down to the grass airstrip outside of town. The surge of her blood in her veins, the buzzing in her stomach as the plane's nose pointed down at the ground and the spectators rushed up at them, and the hook was sunk. She would fly.

There was a picture of her mother on the dresser, the last one before the typhus took her. Her mother had been kind and soft spoken in all matters except for schooling. How she had drilled Aubrey in French every weekend. Aubrey's father had met Celine de Ferrière in Montreal in 1908 and brought his new wife home to Michigan. Aubrey was born two years later, the only child in a loving marriage.

Complications in the pregnancy had left Celine unable to bring a sister or brother into the world for Aubrey. Those complications had also weakened her. When the typhus came, it was that much easier for it to carry her off.

There was one more photo on the dresser: a young woman, probably her own age. Dark hair, a simple ribbon tied around her forehead, and a sweater. She was sitting on some stone steps, her hands folded in her lap, a dismayed look on her face. She wasn't looking at the camera but off into the distance. It was the picture the dying man on that Belgian field had given her. His blood still stained the edges. On the back was written *Lydia Frick, Wannsee.*

Aubrey had forgotten all about the picture until she'd shoved her hand into her pocket on the Paris-bound train. For no earthly reason, she'd kept it. When she got back home, she'd found a simple tin frame in the five-and-dime and put it on her dresser. Her father had never seen it; he never came in the room. Aubrey had memorized the writing on the back. She'd also memorized the name of the person the dying man had mentioned: Lazarus. She fell back asleep, staring at the mystery girl with the dark hair and drab sweater.

Aubrey Endeavours was leading Fergie, her four-year-old Bay, from the barn when there was the sound of a car coming up the gravel driveway. She shielded her eyes as the vehicle approached. It was a Dodge, painted in drab military grey. There were numbers stencilled on the fender and a young man behind the wheel; a figure cast in shadow sat in the back. A government car, way out here in Michigan? It could only be one person.

Arthur Colins, her father's closest friend. They had been comrades in the war; he was Uncle Arthur to Aubrey. She felt a flutter of excitement as she watched the car approach. It was Arthur who had brought to her the proposition of flying in the European air rally. Her father had given her a skeptical look when she'd mentioned it later, after Arthur had left. It was only later, when she'd signed on, that Arthur had briefed her on the true nature of the mission. He'd given her the opportunity to back out, but she had not taken it.

When she returned home from Europe, her father had been grateful she was unhurt but had shown little interest in her exploits. She had shown him a clipping from the *London Times* and had given him the carefully prepared cover story: she'd got as far as Germany; her plane had suffered mechanical failure at the Belgium border. She had been forced to withdraw. "Mechanical failure" – yeah, right, she thought. The borrowed plane had been deliberately set ablaze by that cold British gentlemen she'd had the displeasure of meeting. She'd never learned his name.

And here Arthur was again, and in a government car no less. This was official business. Aubrey ran over and hugged him as he climbed out. His embrace was strong, and he smelled of Jockey Club by Floris, a scent he and her father had taken a liking to in Europe. They'd brought a case of it back with them.

"And how are you, my dear?"

"I'm fine, Uncle Arthur."

He held her back at arms' length to take a good look. She was wearing a light-yellow riding jacket, jodhpurs and leather boots, and wore her brown curly locks in a tight bun. "This getup suits you," he told her, "almost as much as a flying suit."

She turned on one foot in a mock pose. Then on impulse, she hugged him again and kissed his ear. "Good to see you."

Ferguson whinnied loudly and stomped the concrete floor of the barn with his hoof.

"How is Fergie?"

"His ears went back when you drove in."

"He's the smartest horse I've ever seen. If you hadn't taken up flying, you could have been a world-famous trick rider on him and toured with Buffalo Bill Cody."

"That's a little before my time."

She took his arm and guided him to the house. Arthur's driver, an army corporal, leaned up against the car and lit a smoke.

"A government car and a uniformed driver," Aubrey said.

"Yes. I'm here on official business, but I should say hello to your father first."

"He's in his study."

They entered the house to the sound of one last annoyed whinny from Ferguson.

"I shouldn't keep you from your ride."

"Nonsense. Fergie has me every day." She took Arthur's hat and led him to her father.

Colonel Endeavours was in the study, stretched out in a cane-backed chair, his favourite. A blanket lay over his legs and a book had fallen open on his lap. The sound of his snoring filled the room as they entered.

"Dad... Father."

She shook him. "Dad, I've got a big surprise. Please wake up."

"Huh," the colonel said, and his eyes slowly opened. He saw Aubrey first and then the guest.

"What the devil is he doing here? Aubrey, you let this scoundrel in our house?"

"I had no choice, Father. He had a gun on me."

"Why, you," he said, and rose from his chair. His face broke into a grin as Arthur Colins and he shook hands.

"Good to see you, Arthur. You get lost or something?"

"Yes. I took a left turn out of crazy town and wound up here. Paradise."

"It used to be."

The farm had been in the Endeavours family for generations. Aubrey's grandfather had invested well in oil and built a magnificent farmhouse with a wraparound porch where the original, two-room homestead had been.

Then the grandfather had blown it all in the recession of 1903. He'd nearly lost the farm, then had nearly lost it again during the Depression when brown rust had destroyed the wheat and corn had hit rock bottom. If it were not for Aubrey's prize money from her flying, they would have lost it all. That source of income had ended when Aubrey had crashed and totalled her plane. What little compensation she'd received from Arthur after the European escapade, by way of a middleman, was nearly gone as well.

"Aubrey, will you excuse us?" Arthur asked.

"He's here on official business," Aubrey told her father. "I'll post a guard at the door."

Arthur smiled weakly at the joke. "Can you give my driver a glass of water or lemonade? We've had a long drive."

"What about you?"

Arthur eyed the decanter of whisky and the other spirits on the side bar. "I'll manage on my own."

"At this hour?"

"It's five o'clock in Paris," Colonel Endeavours said.

"Very well, Father, but don't get drunk. We have to go into town later."

"Out of here, you," the colonel said.

Aubrey paused at the door. "I'll see you before you go, Arthur?"

"Count on it," he said.

She poured the driver a glass of fresh lemonade and took it out to him; he was most grateful. Then she went back to the barn and finished tacking up Ferguson. She could take him out for a long ride, she knew; she was confident Arthur wouldn't leave without seeing her. She climbed up into the saddle and was starting down the worn trail when she spotted the postal delivery boy on his bicycle at the end of the driveway. He was putting something in their roadside mailbox.

Ferguson protested when she steered him away from the trail that led to the woods on the far side of the farm. She pointed him down the dusty road to the mailbox, then slid out of the saddle and reached in. There were four letters. Aubrey was about to tuck them into the inside pocket of her riding jacket when she noticed one of them was addressed to her. That was unusual. She had written a cousin in Canada a few times, mostly just to practice her written French, but that had trailed off after the war. This letter looked official; the address was typed. The return address was New York. She tore into it and read the letter while Ferguson stomped beside her.

"Oh my," she said, and Ferguson whickered in response.

"There, there, Ferguson. We'll go riding later. I have to speak to Father." She galloped back to the house, the letter fluttering in the wind like she was a runner delivering an important message from headquarters to the front lines.

The army driver was back in the car, the windows rolled down. He sat motionless, staring straight ahead while she hurriedly untacked Ferguson and put him back in his stall.

The empty glass was sitting on the porch railing, and she took it inside, the letter still in her hand. She read it once again, slower this time to make sure she got it right. It was from the Lux Corporation. They had reviewed her request for sponsorship and were happy to announce that they wanted her for a cross-country six-week advertising campaign. They would contact her soon for details.

Aubrey could envision herself flying into small town fairs, her new plane painted with Lux Soap on the side. That would seem tacky, but anything to get back up into the air again. She wondered how much they would sponsor her for and what plane she could afford. There was a monthly newsletter on planes for sale, but her subscription had lapsed. After her crash in Ohio, she hadn't seen the point. The depression she'd fallen into had left her with an understanding of what her father was going through, if only in minuscule proportion.

She would have to see about renewing her subscription. The address was upstairs in her room. She could rip off a letter and get it to them when she and her father went into town. She would also cable back a reply to the Lux Corporation; she wouldn't waste time with ordinary mail. Their proposal demanded immediate response despite the cost of a telegram, lest they find some other fabulous aviatrix to sell their soap nationwide. "Get on it, Aubrey," she told herself.

The double doors of her father's study were flung open, startling her. Colonel Endeavours led Arthur Colins into the kitchen.

"Mail, Father." She handed him the other three letters. He scarcely glanced at them.

"Aubrey, Arthur here wants to—"

"And this came, too." She giddily handed him the letter from New York. He ignored it as well.

"Read it, Father. It's from the Lux Corporation, out of New York, no less," she said, and winked at Arthur.

"Aubrey..."

"They want to sponsor me—a huge nationwide campaign. I'm going to get another airplane. Isn't that great?"

"Aubrey, please listen to me," her father said. "Arthur here wants to talk to you."

"Sure. But read the letter, please."

"Aubrey, damn you—listen. Enough about the Lux Corporation and airplanes. Arthur has come all this way to speak to you."

"Eddie, it's okay," Arthur said placatingly. "Aubrey is excited. Maybe I should come back later. I'm in town for the night."

"Nonsense. You'll stay here."

"It wouldn't be appropriate."

"I'm sorry, Uncle Arthur," said Aubrey. "We can chat. I just got caught up in the whole thing. We can go out on the porch."

"Maybe a walk would be better," Arthur suggested.

"Sure, if you want. I'll grab my hat."

Her father retreated to his study and left them to it.

The cloud cover from the morning had vanished, leaving a striking blue sky and blazing sun. It was warm out amongst the growing corn with no shade whatsoever. Aubrey finally focused on her uncle, forgetting momentarily about the exciting news from New York.

"How is your father?" Arthur said. They were a hundred feet from the house, past the barn, walking slowly. They heard Ferguson; she'd get to him later, right after Arthur left. She would ride out the excitement of the news from New York and spend every minute she could attending to her beloved friend before she left.

"Father is okay, I guess."

"Really?"

"No," she admitted. "He's changed. He doesn't speak much to me or to the Millersons," she said, meaning their next-door neighbours. "He doesn't seem to have any interest in anything at all anymore."

"Just getting old."

"You and he are the same age. Are you losing interest in things?"

"Heavens, no. I never stop. I've got more work than I can handle. Which brings me to why I'm here. Aubrey, I didn't come just to pay a call on your father. It's you I came to talk to. We were very impressed with your trip to Europe. The things you did, what you went through. The way you handled yourself. The report was most impressive." He shook his head. "Your father would kill me if he knew what we'd gotten you involved with."

"I'll never tell. I know how important it is I keep it a secret. You can count on me."

"I know I can. That's why I want you to come work for me."

"What?" She stopped dead in her tracks. "For the army?"

"I'm not really in the army anymore. It's just a courtesy rank; helps cut through the red tape in Washington. I'm with the government."

"I figured as much. That mission I went on was top secret. What government work, then? Are you a G-man? That's exciting."

Along with the newsreels she'd seen about Nazi Germany, there had also been plenty of press on the formation of the Federal Bureau of Investigation, led by J. Edgar Hoover. The whole country was captivated by Hoover's personal war on crime. Dillinger, Baby Face Nelson, Machine Gun Kelly. She knew all their names.

"No, I'm in intelligence."

"Spies. Like that British fellow I met in Belgium."

He chuckled and they continued walking. He shoved his hands in his pockets and kicked at a clump of dirt.

"He was quite impressed with you as well."

"Wish I could say it was mutual."

"An agent in the field is under a lot of pressure. I've known him a long time, Aubrey. He's a good man."

"I'll take your word for it. So, what sort of work do you do?"

"The prevailing attitude in Washington is that gentlemen don't read other gentlemen's mail."

"Is that what you do, steam open letters?"

"Not quite. But our attitude to spying is changing. It has to. Most nations, both our friends and our enemies, are engaged in espionage. You speak French, don't you?"

"Fluently. Mother tutored me every day."

"I never quite picked it up while I was overseas with your father. He, on the other hand..."

"Mother tutored him too."

"Good."

"You were saying something about our enemies?"

"They employ intelligence-gathering against us. The Brits have been reading other gentlemen's mail for centuries, and they're quite good at it. They're 'bringing us along,' a phrase they would use. We're the juniors in this new venture, so we need bringing along."

"I see. I have to admit, what I did in Germany for you—"

"It was for your country."

"Right. It was very thrilling, dangerous. Reminded me of old times, flying through a thunderstorm or going over the Rockies. But that letter from the Lux Corporation—it's a new start, a new plane. It's going to get me back," she pointed at the sky, "up there."

"I see, Aubrey. I understand. You were born to soar. The question is where and for whom." He stopped walking and patted her shoulder. "Well, I must go, I have a telephone call to make."

"We have a phone in the house."

"Official business, I'm afraid. I can't call from here. You and your father are going into town later today?"

"Yes."

"Why not join me for dinner at my hotel? I'm staying at the Birchmount."

"We'll meet you there, say five o'clock?"

"You seemed relieved."

"Do I? Its just..." She trailed off.

"Tell me."

"I thought you were going to propose."

That caught Arthur off guard, and he blushed. She'd never seen a reaction like that from him. Then he started to laugh and she joined him in the joke.

"You know, that's not a bad idea, but in the end, I don't think we'd be well suited."

She hooked her arm in his and steered him back to the house. "Why's that?"

"You're too much of a free spirit, like me. Your father never could rein me in when I served with him. A union between the two of us? I'd have the same difficulty. Maybe it would be just punishment."

They laughed all the way back to the house. As they approached, they saw Colonel Endeavours standing in the front window, holding onto an empty whisky glass. Their laughter fell off as they saw his face. He was looking through them, like they weren't there. It was a terrified, vacant look.

"Oh, dear. He looks terrible," Aubrey whispered.

"He's back there, Aubrey. Back in France, at least in his mind. It's my fault. I started him drinking when I arrived." He looked at the colonel, then back at Aubrey. "Does he do that often? Stare like that?"

"I don't know," she said, and suddenly the letter from Lux and Arthur Colins' offer of employment seemed ugly. She would be leaving her father when he needed her the most.

Colonel Endeavours appeared to have recovered when they walked into the house. He came out of the study and said goodbye to his friend after confirming that he and Aubrey would be in town later and would meet him for supper.

After Arthur had driven off, Aubrey went over to her father and asked him if he was feeling alright.

"Just fine," he said. "We only had the one scotch."

Aubrey nodded. "Was there anything you wanted to talk about?"

"What did you think of his proposal?"

"He told you?"

"Said he had work for you. For a second I thought he was going to ask my permission to marry you."

"Funny, I thought the same thing."

"So, about the job?"

"He couldn't give me a lot of details."

"That's the nature of his work. You'll understand if you agree to it."

"What do you think I should do?"

"There's nothing like serving your country, Aubrey, even in some small part. It fills you with a feeling of accomplishment, of pride."

Edmundson Endeavours looked back into his study, toward the window. Aubrey followed his gaze.

"Father," she said gently, "we saw you standing there. It was like you were someplace else."

"I saw him—Arthur—out there walking, and it brought back a memory is all. It's over now, past. What's in the past remains there."

Her father called to her just after lunch. They had to hurry; the bank closed at three. While he got the Ford started up, she went into the barn to see about Ferguson. He nickered while she rubbed his muzzle, scratched his blaze.

The ride to town was half an hour. They turned out of the drive and passed by the Millerson homestead, but saw no one in the front acreage. Aubrey decided that before she went away on her promotional tour, she would have to stop in there and talk to Hillary Millerson about her father, ask her to watch over the place—and him. She made a mental note to be honest with Mrs. Millerson. She was going to tell her all about her father; the peculiar spells of late. The drinking.

The town of Sacred was home to two thousand people. The main street was bustling with cars and pedestrians. They found a parking spot right in front of the bank. Aubrey and her father split up in front of it. She explained that she had to visit the post office and Western Union. He was going to the bank and then the John Deere dealership to see about a part for their tractor. They would meet up later in the lobby of Arthur's hotel at the end of the main strip.

Aubrey had a letter to the airplane magazine all made out, with a cheque enclosed; she just needed a stamp. After that was taken care of and the letter was on its way, she crossed the street to the Western Union office, where she paid three dollars and twenty cents to send an expedited telegram to the Lux Corporation. She couldn't contain the joy she felt when she handed the card across to the telegraph operator. It was a fella she'd gone to school with, Kevin Baker.

"New York city, huh, Aubrey?" Kevin said.

"You bet; they're going to send me around the country. I'll be getting a plane again."

"Try not to crash it this time. My father says you were lucky to live through that."

She stuck her tongue out at him. "Don't worry, I'll buzz your house when I get it. You can come out and watch me fly overhead."

"Just be careful. My father says you were the most famous person from Sacred."

"First off, I don't live in Sacred and I don't consider myself to be *from* Sacred. Our farm is across the town line. I just went to school here. And secondly, what do you mean '*were* the most famous'? Who else you got?"

Kevin stuck his tongue out back at her. Then, their comedy routine over with, he tapped out the telegram and collected the money.

Done earlier than expected, Aubrey sauntered off down the street and ran into her father going into the John Deere shop. She waited outside while he spoke to a salesman he knew. Despite not officially being from Sacred, her father knew every soul in town. He was the second most famous person from the area, she supposed. There was a war memorial in the centre of town with the names of the fourteen boys who had enlisted, including Johnny Millerson, who'd never come back. Those boys should be regarded as the most famous, she thought. Her father would agree.

"Going to take two weeks. Can you believe that?" her father said when he came out of the shop.

"Lucky thing we have a second tractor," Aubrey said. "And the Millersons have one too."

Aubrey felt another sharp pang of guilt. Her father was having problems with the farm, and here she was about to take off on a grand cross-country adventure.

They left the car where it was parked and walked arm in arm down the street toward the Birchmount. As they strolled, Colonel Endeavours greeted several shopkeepers and citizens of Sacred. They all seemed concerned about and interested in Aubrey and how she was making out after her crash.

"I just wish everyone would stop talking about it," she told her father when they were alone again.

"People were worried about you."

"Were you worried?"

"Of course. Those flying contests, that barnstorming—they put you in awful situations, made you do foolish things."

"You think I was being foolish when I crashed?"

"I know all about violent down-drafts. Been caught in a couple myself." He looked at her sharply.

"Of course, Father. I didn't mean anything by that."

He hugged her closer. "You survived. That's the main thing."

"And now I'm about to get another plane and do it all over again."

He cleared his throat. "About that. I read the letter a couple of times, Aubrey. I didn't read where it says you'll be flying. It doesn't say anything about an airplane."

"What else would they want an aviator for, other than to have her do what she does best?"

"Just don't get your hopes up. Arthur's offer doesn't interest you?"

"It does interest me, but my heart and soul belong in the sky."

"There's no future in it, kiddo. In a couple of years no one will care about female flyers. You're just a flash in the pan."

"We're becoming commercial pilots," she protested. "Soon we'll be flying people all around the country, and there's always the mail service."

"Forget about that, Aubrey. Please. I don't want you flying through some blizzard up in Alaska."

"I'm just saying it's opening up a whole world of opportunity for women. Things are changing. We've had the right to vote for fifteen years, Father. Has the whole world collapsed as you predicted?"

"No, not yet," he said, and pulled her off balance in an attempt to make her laugh.

"It's true, Father. You'll see."

They reached the hotel and saw Arthur seated inside the dining room. He raised his coffee cup at them.

"Think there's coffee in that?" Aubrey whispered to her father. "I mean, Prohibition has ended; you don't have to hide it anymore."

"This hotel is dryer than dirt. It was before Prohibition, and it is now. Don't know why he chose it."

"Maybe loose lips from alcohol, him being a spy and all." She gave him a cheeky grin.

"I wouldn't go around repeating that. He wouldn't like it."

"Right. My lips are sealed."

Arthur Colins met the two Endeavours halfway and escorted them to his table. He ordered coffees for them. "I have a five-thirty reservation for dinner," he told them when the waiter had departed.

"That's fine," Colonel Edmundson said.

Arthur turned his attention to Aubrey. "Did you get your errands in town done?"

"I did. I ripped off a letter to the magazine, the one that advertises planes for sale. And I sent a telegram to New York accepting their offer. I just have to wait for the details now."

Arthur didn't show any disappointment. He just nodded, a thin smile on his lips.

"I think she's a damn fool," Edmundson broke in. It didn't dent Aubrey's enthusiasm one bit, but Arthur scolded him with a look.

"She can make up her own mind."

"A job with the government is security, and it's rewarding," the colonel went on, undeterred. "You saw what happened to her last time she flew. She almost died."

Of course, the colonel was talking about the last race Aubrey had entered, not the adventure she'd had recently in Europe. That had never been revealed to him; as far as he knew, Aubrey had entered the race and withdrawn due to mechanical issues. As for the truth, he had no need to know. Aubrey didn't agree with that, but she had promised Arthur she would not reveal what had really happened over there, to anyone, ever.

"It'll be all right, Father," she said. "I'll be flying from town to town, showing off my gams and flashing eyes at the photographers to sell a few bars of soap. Nothing to worry about."

"I bet," Arthur said. "When you crashed, were you attempting to fly across the Rockies?"

"Uh-huh. It was a race—fastest time over the hump. Women only."

The colonel looked absently out the hotel window and said, "It's all just a load of guff. Women flyers." He harrumphed. "They're just using you to promote their newspapers or sell their products."

"That's right, and I'm going to use them to get my next plane. I'm not flying blind in this." Arthur smiled at her joke. "I know what I'm doing. I've set my course and I intend to fly it. Sure, I might get sidetracked a few times. Who knows which way the wind blows?" She paused. "Actually, I do – sometimes straight down. But I can handle it." She put a hand on her father's knee and squeezed it.

"Come on, you two," Arthur said, getting to his feet. "Let's see if they're ready for us in the restaurant."

Colonel Endeavours was right: even though Prohibition had been repealed two years earlier, there wasn't a drop of alcohol on the menu. Aubrey knew the family that owned the hotel; they were strict Quakers. She didn't mind. Alcohol weakened her flying skills; she had to keep them sharp. She could drink with the best of them, but abstained most of the time.

After their lovely meal of lamb with cranberry and asparagus, the two Endeavours said goodbye to Arthur Colins. He had an early train out of Sacred, bound for Detroit. He didn't mention his ultimate destination, and Aubrey had learned not to pry. Her father certainly didn't pry. It gave Arthur Colins an aura of mystery she found alluring. She thought again about the funny coincidence earlier: she and her father thinking the same thing about Arthur Colins and a marriage proposal.

They arrived back home at sundown and she saw to Ferguson one last time, kissing him on his mane and then retiring for the night. Her father stayed up listening to the radio and undoubtedly draining some of his stash of scotch. She bid him goodnight and climbed the stairs to her room.

The scream broke into her dreams, turning it nightmarish. She thrashed in bed and launched herself bolt upright. Her forehead was covered in a thin sheen of sweat and she clutched at her pounding heart. Had the scream come from her while she slept? The bedroom window was open; a moist breeze engulfed the room. Had it been thunder? Her heart was pounding; she had no recollection of the crashing dream. She was just about to lie back down when she heard it again.

"No!" the shout from her father's room thundered down the hall. "No, Allan, don't! Get down!"

She was out of bed like a shot, running down the hall to his room. She forced herself to pause at the bedroom door and cracked it open. Her father was kneeling in the middle of the bed, the sheets scrunched up under his chin, spreading out like a tent.

"No, Allan, you promised. I don't want you to. Get down, everyone. Down!"

Aubrey's heart sank, seeing her father so distressed. She walked softly into the bedroom and approached him cautiously. Then she saw the gun in his hand. Edmundson Endeavours whirled, pointed it in her direction and fired. The shot from the .45

splintered the wood panelling a foot from Aubrey's head.

"Who's there? Hun bastards!" Colonel Endeavours pulled the hammer back, ready to fire again.

"Father its me—Aubrey." She ducked down, but he followed her with the business end of the .45. He couldn't see her, but he could hear her.

"Daddy, don't! It's me."

"Celine?" He called out. Aubrey's mother.

"No, Father, it's Aubrey. Your daughter."

"Aubrey?" The colonel sank back on the bed. He let the sheets fall down from his face. The hand holding the .45 went slack and fell limply onto the mattress. Aubrey leapt up and grabbed the revolver from him. She tossed it into the corner and went to her weeping father.

"Oh, Aubrey, Aubrey," the colonel moaned. "I'm so glad to see you. Where have you been?"

"Here, Father. I've been here all along."

He stroked her hair and hugged her tight. She felt his tears soaking into her nightdress and cried along with him.

Afterwards, when he was fully awake and breathing normally, Aubrey turned on the lights and he saw the bullet hole. His face turned pale with horror. Then he saw the gun in the corner and he clamped a hand over his mouth as though he were going to be sick. Aubrey went to it.

"Careful with that," he said automatically, then looked away from her, stricken. "Who am I to talk, eh? What kind of father almost shoots his own daughter?"

43

"Do you remember the dream?"

He nodded. "Same one every night. A Kraut air raid on our forward camp. Caught us on the ground, chewed up four of our planes." He wiped away a tear and his lips trembled.

She sat on the edge of the bed again, but put the gun behind her. She would deal with that later.

"Who is Allan?"

"A replacement pilot. I never got to know him. You didn't want to—you understand? He didn't last a week. Never had the chance to learn. I never had the chance to teach him." He looked past her at the gun. "Damn it, I almost killed you."

"I'm taking this gun out of here." She got to her feet.

"A good idea. I need a drink."

"I think that's part of the problem. You should quit it, Father. What would Mother say?"

"She'd call me *un vieil imbécile*, an old fool."

His imitation of his wife was spot on, and Aubrey laughed. He grinned, despite himself. She flicked off the light.

"Try and get some sleep."

"The sheet is soaking wet."

"I'll open the window. It'll dry." She left him with his nightmares, the .45 firmly in her hand. She unloaded it and made it safe before putting it away in her nightstand. Her father had taught her how to shoot and handle guns since an early age; she had a healthy respect for them.

She also knew that he could not be near that firearm anymore. That was the gun he'd carried to war and back, but it must be taken away now, she decided; sold or buried in the field. They had no need for firearms out here. There was an old shotgun above the fireplace, but the shells were long gone. Her father had given up hunting when he came back from the war. He told her he'd killed enough and he was ashamed. He'd kept the .45 for sentimental reasons only. She opened the nightstand drawer and looked at the gun, then closed the drawer again, undecided. Maybe he could have it back, if she just removed the bullets from the clip. She would discuss it with him tomorrow when he was calm again.

Aubrey encouraged Ferguson over the last jump. They'd been set up years ago, three jumps spaced along the riding path through the clump of woods at the edge of their property. She would take Ferguson through the jumps, turn him around and do them on the way back. He needed no encouragement. Glad to have her on his back, Ferguson carried her triumphantly through the forest. She'd gotten up early, and now she caught the morning dew on the lily pads by the pond as she thundered by on her steed.

She slowed Ferguson to a trot on the way back up to the house. She saw the Western Union truck in the driveway, the uniformed delivery man coming down the steps. Her father was standing in the doorway, reading the telegram. She goosed a bit more out of Ferguson and cantered into the paddock.

The truck had already turned around and was speeding off by the time she'd placed Ferguson in front of the trough and hurried over to her father. She took off her elbow-length leather gloves and her father looked down at her from the porch.

"Is that what I think it is?" she asked breathlessly. "Of course it is. It's from New York, isn't it?"

"It is."

"You read it?"

"Sure. I signed for it. It was just marked 'Endeavours.'" He looked sheepish.

"Oh, Father. I don't mind." She climbed the steps, hand outstretched. Colonel Endeavours hesitated, then handed the yellow card over.

She read it fast. Her face, at first ablaze with excitement, suddenly turned sour.

"I'm sorry, Aubrey. I know it wasn't what you were hoping for. Still, it's a job. It might lead to other things."

She fanned herself with the card. The words on it were ringing in her head. Details on the promotion, a flat refusal to finance a plane, the tour to be conducted by train, forty-five cities in six weeks. Reimbursement for expenses only, minimal daily stipend. Maybe that's why her father was now keen on her accepting it: there would be no flying.

"I'd hardly call that a job. They pay for my train tickets and meals. Big deal."

"It could lead to other opportunities. You'd be famous again."

"Hardly—selling soap out of the back of someone's pickup. Me and bunch of other hotty-totties strutting our stuff in swimwear. No thanks. Not this gal." Suddenly, her face brightened. "When was Uncle Arthur's train?"

Colonel Edmundson checked his watch. "Leaves in forty-three minutes."

"The truck..."

"I drained the oil overnight. I'd have to fill it."

"No time."

There was a whinny behind her. She tucked the envelope in her pocket as she sprinted for Ferguson. He seemed delighted with the unexpected ride as she swung herself up into the saddle. She put the reins to him crossways across his neck like she'd seen Tom Mix do in the movies and galloped down the driveway.

4

Arthur Colins's driver brought the drab grey government-issued Dodge around to the front of the Birchmount. He jumped out of the car and snapped to attention as Colins emerged carrying a suitcase and leather-bound grip. As the driver took the luggage from Colins, there was the sound of a horse's hooves at a gallop on the paved main street. It had been a dirt track up until ten years before; there were still a few hitching posts along the sidewalk.

Arthur's jacket was thrown over his shoulder; he held an unlit cigarette between his lips. He looked up from lighting it as Aubrey brought Ferguson to a halt in front of the hotel, caught the reins and put the cigarette back in its case.

"Aubrey, you devil, flying down the street like a banshee."

She was out of breath, almost as much as Ferguson was. A country boy from Kansas himself, Arthur lashed the reins to a fencepost while she caught her breath.

"Thought I missed you," she told him.

"You almost did. Corporal McWilliams here was going to drive me to the train station. I'm on the Red Ball to Detroit. Sorry, but we have to get going."

"That job offer—I want it, if it's not filled."

Arthur chuckled again. "It's not filled. You only turned me down last night. Why the change of heart?"

"I'm free. My circumstances have been altered. I'm all yours."

"And the next flying promotional tour that comes your way? You're not going to abandon me halfway through this thing, are you?"

"No, sir. Those swine, the Lux Corporation. They don't want my flying skills, just my girlish good looks." She struck a pose and went sweet. Arthur didn't bite,

"I'm serious, Aubrey. Are you committed to this? I dare say it's a good deal more important than any soap-selling promotion."

"I promise. They cabled me this morning. I'm not even going to bother to reply. They can get some cutie anywhere. So, what do you say?"

Arthur reached into his pocket and retrieved a paper folder, the kind they tucked train tickets into. He handed it to her and pulled her away from Corporal McWilliams.

"You're on the Red Ball to Detroit—same one I'm on, only two days from now. Gives you time to get sorted and say goodbye to your father."

At the mention of her father, a frown creased her face. She'd almost forgotten the horrific episode last night. By all rights, if he'd had better aim when he was half asleep, she should be dead. The gun was still in her nightstand.

Arthur looked at her. "What's the matter? Is he alright?"

"He's fine. I'll talk to him about this. Detroit and then where? You weren't finished."

"And then a connecting train to New York. I need you there no later than the twenty-ninth."

"For what?"

"For your briefing. After you sign your life away to me and Uncle Sam, that is." He handed over the ticket. "Pack for a three-week trip. Plenty of warm clothes and then some nice evening wear, I'd suggest."

"Really?" She gave him a dubious look. "I don't have anything like that. I wear pants mostly. Comfortable for flying."

"There's a bank draft in there for expenses. Use some of it to get fixed up."

"In Sacred? Hardly."

"New York, then. They have stores there, you know."

"Don't I know it." She grinned. "Okay, fantastic. I'll meet you where?"

"The details are in there. First thing you learn, Aubrey: when working for me, when we're out in public, you keep your mouth shut."

The seriousness of his tone shocked her. She nodded. "Uh-huh. Got it."

"Fine. Now, take this horse home and say goodbye to him. Tell your dad another goodbye from me. Tell him I'll take care of you. You won't be able to write or make any phone calls for a while, but I'll keep in touch."

"Okay, Uncle Arthur."

"And it's Walton, John Walton, from here on out. It's called a work name. You'll understand after the twenty-ninth."

50

"Right, Mr. Walton." She watched him drive away from the hotel and then remounted Ferguson.

"Come along, Fergie. We'll take it nice and slow on the way home. Good boy."

Aubrey did indeed take her time getting home. She went by way of the Western Union office, where she paid seventy-nine cents to send a three-word reply to the Lux Corporation: Offer politely declined. She rode slowly the rest of the way home, though her mind and heart were racing ahead of her by a mile.

"You catch him?" her father asked when she came into his study. He was sipping a coffee and watching one of the Millerson boys plow the back forty. He had a brass telescope set up for that purpose.

"I did indeed."

"When do you leave?"

"In two days. Mr. Wal—" She had been about to use his workname but caught herself in time. Her father gave her a sharp look.

"It's a shifty business he's in. My advice to you is to get in, make some money, polish your typing skills and then get out. The whole world is opening up for you, Aubrey, and you'll make some good contacts. Just don't get sucked too deeply into Arthur's world."

"What did Uncle Arthur do for you in the army? You never told me. I mean, I know he was in G2, whatever that was."

"He was in Army Intelligence, assigned to the Air Service. He ran spies in France and Belgium that provided intelligence on the targets we hit. And since we're sharing here, what did he have you do over there?"

Aubrey breathed in deeply. She was about to break her promise to Arthur Colins.

"I had to fly over Germany and land in a field. Pick someone up."

"I see. Dangerous?"

She remembered the stuttering sound of the machine gun fire from the fighters. The evil glow of the green tracers, fingers of death reaching out for her. And she remembered vividly the man whose hand she'd held in that field in Belgium.

"No. Piece of cake. Arthur said it was going to be routine, and he was true to his word." She had at least kept part of the promise.

"Germany? Do you have any idea how dangerous that was?"

"It was a one-off thing. Like you said, this time I'm probably going to be polishing my typing skills."

"Let's hope so."

Aubrey daydreamed while she set out clothes to take on her trip to New York. She went to the nightstand to retrieve her diary and saw the Colt .45 sitting on top of it. The magazine with its copper-tipped bullets lay next to it. She picked the weapon up. Its weight gave it a certain confidence and character all its own. She knew she could put a round into a target a hundred feet away with a fair degree of accuracy, and with a rifle she was even better. She hefted the weapon in her hand, thought about it here in the house alone with her father. He might find it and reload it: 'Not much good if it isn't loaded,' he always said. And then one night when he was in the dark place, back there on the airfield in France or flying behind enemy lines, and the ghosts of the dead

52

he'd left behind came out to haunt him, what would he do with it? Would he merely put another bullet into the bedroom wall, or do something worse?

She shuddered. The weapon should be disposed of, given away, perhaps handed over to the Millersons for safekeeping. But that would not be much better; what if one of their grandkids picked it up and played with it? Okay, well, maybe she could bury it in a field. Again, she hesitated; for some reason the gleaming black weapon didn't deserve a fate as ignominious as that. It had served her father well during the war. In the end, she carried it and the magazine down to the kitchen and put them in a large counter jar her mother had used for flour.

For a brief moment, she dreamt of riding in train carriages and love affairs with dark-haired, exotic agents. Were such things possible? Childish, schoolgirl fantasies, she finally concluded and chided herself. She had no idea what her uncle Arthur, now Mr. John Walton, had in store for her. But she was eager to find out.

5

John Walton was there on the platform in Penn Station when Aubrey arrived. He took her single suitcase and led her to a waiting taxi.

"No car, no driver this time?"

Walton smiled. "Too conspicuous here in New York. Too impractical. I find the subway a lot easier to get around."

The taxi took them over to the Piedmont Hotel, where Aubrey had a room booked for her. She was checked in and left on her own for an hour. Walton had to attend to something, he said, but would be back to collect her.

He was punctual; there was rap on her door at the sixty-minute mark. She let her uncle in. He had someone with him, a smaller man, glasses, rather bookish. He looked like an accountant.

"Aubrey, this is Carson. He's with me."

The man did not offer to shake hands, just nodded perfunctorily and went to the small table in the room. He had a briefcase with him and he set it on the table and opened it. A pile of papers was spread out on the bed.

Arthur said, "We want you to read these, Aubrey. These are terms of employment. They're mandatory, I'm afraid."

She picked up the papers and glanced through them. They were legal contracts of some kind.

"They're an acknowledgement that you have read the *Espionage Act* of 1917. That you swear an oath of allegiance to this country, promise not to betray her to a foreign power."

"But Unc—Mr. Walton. Haven't I already proven my loyalty?"

"It's necessary, Aubrey, before we brief you on your first mission."

"Doesn't sound like I'm being sent off to the steno pool," she quipped.

"Gosh, no," Walton said, raising his eyebrows. "Go ahead—read them thoroughly and sign if you want to continue. If you don't, I have return tickets to Michigan. No hard feelings."

"Pen," Aubrey said. Carson produced one and Aubrey rifled through the papers to the final one and signed it. She handed them back to Carson along with the pen.

"I'm in."

"Excellent. Carson, over to you."

John Walton went over to the window and looked down on Manhattan while Carson talked to her for the next hour.

"You want me to go back?" Aubrey said when he was finished.

"Yes," Carson said.

"To Germany? I barely made it out alive the first time."

Carson looked embarrassed. Maybe he wasn't privy to the details of the operation to lift that spy out of the Nazi Reich. She didn't give a damn.

Walton spoke up. "This will be different. Nothing dangerous, I promise. All we want you to do is attend this aviation exhibition. The Germans are anxious to show off their tremendous leaps forward in aeronautics. You'd be representing the United States."

"Me? Little old me?"

"You're a celebrity in Germany."

"Oh, come on."

"It's true."

John Walton produced a glossy magazine with German writing on it. It had a picture of Hitler on the cover, naturally. He flipped to the middle of the magazine.

"There's an article here about you; nice picture. Women flyers are celebrities in Europe. You must have experienced some of that when you were in Poland."

"True." She wouldn't admit it, but she had loved the attention the Poles had lavished on her. "But surely someone bigger than me could go. Maybe Earhart? She *did* solo the Atlantic."

"We tried. Her husband, Putnam, that hustler, has his eyes set on bigger things for her. Hollywood, perhaps. Personally, I think you'd make a bigger splash on the west coast than Amelia Earhart."

"Why, thank you." She mock-preened. "So, what am I supposed to do at this exhibition?"

"Look at the new aircraft Messerschmitt and Focke-Wulf are producing. In particular, the new Bf 109. We know hardly anything about it. It's still in prototype phase, and but it's going to be the main fighter of Hitler's Luftwaffe. We hear it's fast."

"Why do I think there's more to it than that?"

"This operation will be run by the Brits."

Aubrey put her cup down; she remembered the last British intelligence man she'd met.

"Look, they're the best at this sort of thing."

"Thought I was just supposed to look around."

"Maybe take a photo or two. They'll teach you how to do that. Ask the right questions, probe. We want to know about stall rates, rates of climb, fuel consumption, speeds at takeoff, range, armament. This information could be vital in the years to come. You can't deny that you're perfectly suited for this assignment."

"And how am I supposed to get this information out of Germany?"

"The Brits will show you how. We can't expect you to memorize everything."

"When do I leave?"

"Tonight."

"Tonight?"

"You'll catch a steamer to Cherbourg, France. The exhibition just started; you'll be a little late."

"Good planning." She rolled her eyes.

Walton shrugged. "It is what it is."

"Boy, that's clever."

"So..."

"I guess when my country calls, I answer it."

"Fantastic. I have the tickets here. You'll meet a man named Purnsley in Paris. Here are the contact details. Follow them to the letter. You have the rest of the night to memorize them. They'll have to be destroyed afterwards."

"I was supposed to do a little shopping."

"I had one of my girls do it for you. The clothes are in the closet."

"Do I get a code name?"

"No, you're going as Aubrey Endeavours, the famous aviatrix."

"Right, forgot. Aviatrix and spy. What if I get arrested?"

"What for?"

"That earlier trip to Germany," she said.

"They haven't the foggiest that it was you that night. The crash in Belgium—they bought the whole thing. There was an outpouring of relief that you were unhurt. All of Europe expressed it."

"Guess I missed that."

"Don't worry about that. Just concentrate on the job at hand."

"It will be a little difficult. I mean, they did try to kill me; they came awfully close."

"It's the nature of our profession."

Our profession. She liked the sound of that.

She was left alone for an hour. Carson left the Paris contact details for her on the promise that she would burn them in the tub after reading them. They were simple enough; she suspected they were keeping it as uncomplicated as they could for her.

6

John Walton returned alone and got her loaded into the car for the short drive to the New York docks on the East River. The steamer was of the P&O Line, she was booked in tourist class.

"What about salary?" Aubrey said before boarding.

"It's about time you asked me," Walton said.

"You know what? I totally forgot." She'd received a hundred dollars for the snatch job out of Germany.

"You're a freelance journalist. Just starting out in your new career. You've got contracts with several magazines here in the States to publish your articles and your photographs under your own name. Here are the details." He handed her a sheaf of papers. "You can familiarize yourself with them on board."

She flipped through the paperwork, noticed the dates were two weeks old. Were those legitimate or clever forgeries? If they were legitimate, and this thing had been planned weeks in advance, maybe her uncle had had a hand in fending off the Lux Corporation? Nonsense, she told herself. She'd only just told him about that the same day he proposed that she come work for him. He couldn't possibly have that kind of power.

"You will actually have to write a couple of articles and hand over some photographs of German planes and perhaps Berlin to make it legitimate. They'll pay you for them. Journalism is just a cover. In reality, you're working for the State Department. I can't tell you which branch. Officially, we don't exist. You'll be paid by us into a secret bank account. The money will be here waiting for you when you return."

"How much?"

"Five hundred a year."

Aubrey's eyes widened. That was more money than most men made.

"Just don't go flashing it around. Keep it as a nest egg, for when this is all over."

She didn't know what he meant by that, but figured she'd extracted enough info out of him for the time being. They said goodbye at the gangplank that crossed over to the ship. To make it look legitimate they even embraced, just a father seeing his daughter off. Once on deck she made her way to the railing, but John Walton had already left.

The trip was uneventful. They ran into a storm midway across, which sent the passengers to their cabins. She could hear retching from the one next door. A decade of flying had hardened her stomach and she wasn't bothered by rough seas.

They landed at Cherbourg after a seven-day journey and she caught the boat train into Paris. Carson had arranged modest accommodation for her for two nights. Enough time to make contact with her British handler.

She thought of the money the government was paying her. But she also remembered that her father had remarked how the government went back on its word like it was a hobby. But would her uncle go back on his? She didn't think so.

The first order of business was to make that contact with British Intelligence. Her uncle had given her a sketchbook and a set of charcoals and chalk. This was all part of this contact phase: she was to play the part of a tourist. It had been years since she'd last drawn something. Art was never her thing. But she'd practised with the charcoal and chalk while she was on the ship, sketching out a lifeboat and the smoke stacks rising above her on the sun deck.

Now here she was in Paris, with things to sketch all around her. An old woman throwing dirty dish water into the gutter. A vegetable seller pushing a cart loaded with produce. But what was she supposed to draw? She decided on the Eiffel Tower. It was all a ruse, an excuse for her to carry some chalk, which she'd been told she would need when making contact with the Brits.

Walton had called it fieldcraft. There had been a lot to learn and no time to teach her. She would need these skills if she was to successfully go into the Third Reich and make it out again. Thankfully the British would be there to guide her, give her a quick introductory course on being a spy.

She'd watched plenty of spy flicks on the silver screen. *The 39 Steps* was her favourite. And now here she was playing the part. *No, not playing, Aubrey. You are the real deal. Just remember that and you might make it out alive.*

Aubrey took her shoulder bag full of art supplies down to the River Seine and crossed over to the Left Bank. The walkways winding along the river were crowded with artists; it was going to be hard to get a spot to sit. First things first, though. She located the light post at the corner of the Quai D'Orsay and Rue Malar as per her instructions. She held the piece of chalk in her hand down by her side, her bag over her shoulder. She casually walked by the light post and left a streak of white chalk on its blackened metal. She kept moving. Down another block, there was another light post. This time the mark was to be made on the left-hand side. She had to shift the chalk to her other hand. She paused, shielding her eyes from the spring sunshine with her free hand, and left the mark.

There were people everywhere; couples strolling hand in hand; fellow artists and bohemians; men ogling girls. She heard more than one of them call out to her or whistle. She ignored them. With her pantomime done, she found a quiet spot along the Seine and proceeded to play at being the carefree artist, sketching the Eiffel Tower in the distance among the apartment buildings lining the river.

She spent an hour at that, kept it simple: straight lines of the monument, squares for the buildings, lightly shading it in.

"You'll never make it as an artist," she heard someone say behind her in English. Aubrey's heart skipped a beat and her hand started to shake. The final spire of the tower went off at an absurd angle.

"There's always the theatre," she said in reply, without turning. This was the correct phrasing, the challenge and response. Sign, countersign. There was an empty spot on the bench and the man sat down. He wore a brown suit with a Derby, which she knew the British called a bowler. And the man was British; there was no mistaking the accent. He removed his hat to wipe his forehead with his handkerchief.

"There is nothing like a springtime day in Paris, is there?" he said. The second sequence of challenge-and-response phrases.

"It is warm. London is nice too."

"Your marks were not that well done. I could barely see the first one."

"Sorry. My first time," she said while continuing to sketch the tower. The man had not turned to her yet. When he finally did, she took that as a cue that the formalities were over. She looked at him and tried to conceal her shock. It was him—the man from Belgium. The one who had so unceremoniously dumped that poor dead man into the back of the truck. And then dumped her along the side of the road after setting fire to her little Polish airplane.

"Hewitt Purnsley," he said.

"Aubrey Endeavours."

"When you're ready, Miss Endeavours," he said.

She put her things away. "Lead the way."

They walked along the Seine. He put his hand on her back more than once, caressed her shoulder as they paused and looked at Notre Dame cathedral. The touch of his hand on her made her go rock still. She knew it was all an act, pretending to be lovers in the city of love. She found it hard to get used to.

"Have you been fully briefed?"

"Aren't you going to be doing that?"

"Quite. I'm to fill you in on your assignment. But first, there's a few things we have to teach you. Otherwise, you'll just muck it up."

She knew what that meant: arrested for espionage, and by the Gestapo, no less. Not a pleasant prospect.

"If you are to have any chance of succeeding and getting out of there, you'll listen to everything I have to tell you." He pulled a camera out and took pictures. He put it away, and she slipped her hand around his arm and back into her jacket pocket, then rested her head on his shoulder like others were doing.

"Are you always this rude?" she asked.

"If you find me disagreeable, it's because there is so little time. And what I have to teach you will help you survive. Are we clear?"

She lifted her head and removed her hand. To hell with the ruse—boyfriend, girlfriend, two young lovers.

"Whatever you say."

"As I said, we don't have much time. Your training starts now. We're going to walk up this street. I want you to remember every number plate you see. Record them all."

"You mean license plates. That's it? No problem."

They strolled a block. There were trucks and cars, Peugeots and Citroens and large lorries with growling diesel engines belching black smoke. She made a game of it, trying to sing the license plates she saw in her head. They got to the end the block and she started to recite them. She was six into it when she paused and then cautiously carried on. The jocularity of the moment was gone. The look on Purnsley's face told her to be serious. She recounted ten plate numbers correctly.

"You missed two cars."

"Not a bad batting average."

"And you missed the scooters entirely." There had been half a dozen.

"You didn't say scoot—"

"I said number plates. Another block. Try again."

At the end of two hours, Aubrey was exhausted from these memory games. Her last time, she got them all. For the last two plates, she had to dig deep and come up with them even though she'd just seen them.

"You're tired. Long journey. You want to quit?"

She sighed. "I do want a rest."

"You think that's what you'll get out there in the field, in enemy territory—a moment to rest?"

She turned away from him.

"This is important. Remembering a *license* plate will help you spot a tail. It's basic counter-surveillance." He narrowed his eyes at her. "You're not crying, are you?"

"Gosh, no. I wouldn't give you the satisfaction."

He gave a small smile. He'd liked that. "They said you were tough."

"Who did?"

"They. That's all they ever are—just *they*. But if you must know, your man Walton told me how tough you were. Resilient was the word he used. And I saw what you were capable of myself in Belgium. Look, Miss Endeavours, this is standard training. Normally, we would spend a month on this material. I only have you for two days, then I have to send you into Germany. One of the most oppressive and paranoid regimes on the planet."

"I understand. Maybe we could switch it up, try something else."

"Fine. It's getting late. How about dinner first?"

"Come to think of it, yes."

"This is Paris. We should be able to find somewhere decent to eat. But keep your guard up. Your training is not taking a break. The enemy certainly won't."

"Understood."

7

They were halfway through their entrees, stuffed sole for Aubrey, a small braised lamb shank for Hewitt, when he finally had the first serious thing to say to her. They had sipped wine; he had drunk his sparingly, and she had matched his sedate pace. Normally she would have enjoyed a full glass.

"You mustn't get drunk," he told her. "At a cocktail reception or bar, order a club soda with lime by yourself, then when you're with others they'll think it's gin or vodka. Liquor has done in more men in my line than you can imagine."

"When do I get to put it like that?"

"Like what?"

"My line."

"When you've been at it as long as I have."

"And how long has that been?"

"You're prying, Miss Endeavours."

"Just trying to get to know my instructor."

"Since the war."

"Really? You don't look old enough."

"I was eighteen, attached to military intelligence. It was trial by fire back then. Had to learn quickly."

"Like I'm trying to now?"

"Precisely. Bit more at stake back then."

"Where are you from?"

He hesitated, then lowered his shoulders. "Salisbury, west of London. My father is a barrister."

"I think you know a lot about me. Why don't you spill the beans?"

"Right. Aubrey Endeavours. Born in Sacred, Michigan, in 1910. Mother died when you were twelve. Typhus, wasn't it?"

"It was."

"Terrible. Took an uncle of mine and more than one friend in the service. Your father served in the Army Air Service during the war. Distinguished, decorated. Cashiered out a colonel. I bet I know more about his military record than you do."

"Really? Do tell."

"Another time, perhaps. Where was I? You went to the Rockingham Girls' Collegiate. You were asked to leave."

"Kicked out. That's how we would put it in America."

"You caught the flying bug around that time. Learned to fly while working at a five-and-ten store."

"Jerking sodas, cleaning up. Whatever I could. Drove a coal truck one winter."

"Really? That was not in your file. Duly noted. You had the audacity to pick the Pulitzer cross-country air race as your first race. You came in third. You amazed the crowd when you pulled off your flying helmet and revealed that a woman had placed so well. Cheeky," Hewitt said. "I don't understand, though. Weren't there races exclusively for women?"

"There were. I wanted to fly with the boys."

"And a good showing you made, too. Your picture was in papers around the world, including here and in London."

"Those go into your files?"

"That is the mark of a good intelligence agency, the backbone. A good and comprehensive set of files. Your country is just learning that. You've got a lot of catching up to do. What was all that silly nonsense about gentlemen not reading other gentlemen's mail? Time your country grew up. We would have thought your involvement in the war, however brief, would have done that. Looks like it's going to take another dust-up with the Germans to prove the point."

"And files are important to that?"

"We take in everything. Our security service collects information for domestic matters, counter-intelligence and my section."

"And what is that, exactly?"

They were fairly isolated in the restaurant, talking in English and keep their voices low. Not that it mattered what language they were speaking in. The opposition, as Hewitt Purnsley called them, could *sprechen sie Englisch.*

"I'm with His Majesty's Secret Intelligence Service. Also known as MI6. We're responsible for foreign intelligence gathering. I'm a case officer."

"Which means?"

"I run agents."

"Like me."

He chuckled. "No, you're not an agent. A courier, more like. One of ours being sent in. Mostly what I do is identify people on the other side of the fence who want to work for us. Sometimes for money, sometimes for other reasons. I help them out. Those are the spies, really." He pushed his chair back. "Enough of this. I'm going to the facilities. We'll start your next lesson when I get back."

Aubrey finished her Bordeaux; it was the most incredible wine she'd ever had. The waiter came over to clear their plates. She spoke to him in French, but he seemed uninterested in engaging her. Aubrey checked her watch. Hewitt Purnsley had been gone five minutes. Then it became ten. She stared down the short hallway that led to the Ladies and Gents, trying to will him to come out.

She had used the facilities earlier, knew that the hallway led farther into the building, where she had seen stacks of wine cases. The waiter came over with the bill on a silver tray. She glanced at it: 180 Francs. She just might have enough on her. She opened her purse and felt her face flush. Her wallet was gone. She sat there another couple of minutes. The waiter came over again to see if the bill had been paid. It hadn't, and he huffed and stuck his nose in the air.

Finally, she got up and said in French, "I'm going to the ladies. I will settle up when I get back." She took her purse—all it had in it was lipstick and compact—and went down the hallway. She knocked gently on the men's door.

"Hewitt, are you alright?"

No answer. She pushed it open. It was single occupancy and it was empty. She looked nervously down the hallway. There were sounds emanating from the other end, men stacking wooden cases and shouting at each other. That was not a viable exit, at least not for her. He must have gone out that way, but how would she manage it?

She went reluctantly back to her table. The waiter saw her and came over.

"Is there a problem, mademoiselle?"

"Yes. It seems my dinner companion has run off on me."

The waiter remained motionless, unempathetic.

"And my wallet. I seem to have been robbed."

Since they'd sat down, no one had come near their table except their waiter. When she had visited the ladies' room, she had taken her purse with her and remembered seeing the wallet next to her makeup. That could only mean that Hewitt had some how boosted it. But why? Then it clicked: this was the next lesson he'd spoken about. He was forcing her into an uncomfortable position again. But why? To see if she could talk her way out of it? Hardly. No, he was seeing how far she would go, if she would do something she would never have dreamed of before: pull a runner and make a dash for the door. She wouldn't make it out the front door, she knew. The waiter and his co-worker would grab her.

"I'm going to the ladies'; I will settle up when I get back. I don't feel well. If I'm sick, that will determine the gratuity." She didn't run. The men in the back were still there, blocking her way.

"The gratuity is already included, mademoiselle," she heard the man say as she went into the ladies' room again. With the door locked, she started running the water. There was a window up high near the ceiling. She hopped up onto the radiator, grabbed hold of the bar holding the window open and pulled herself up. Her feet scrabbled at the tiled wall. The door handle jiggled.

"Mademoiselle. Are you okay?"

"Not feeling well. I think it was the sole. I knew it had gone off."

The waiter spoke to someone else in French. She caught only part of it: 'the window.' He was sending someone around back to nab her. She had only seconds now. The window opened onto an alley. She pushed herself through head first and crashed down onto more wine crates. The noise she made sounded like gunfire on the Western Front, and she heard a shout from the street. The alley, thankfully, was not a dead end, and she ran off in the opposite direction, her purse flapping wildly against her back.

She dashed out onto a busy street; horns blared as she went into the traffic. She looked back only once to see the waiter's co-worker coming after her, but he bounced off the hood of a slow-moving omnibus and rolled to the ground. She crossed the street and slowed down, fixed her hair and tried to blend into the crowd on the sidewalk. Half a mile up and away from the restaurant, she saw Hewitt Purnsley emerge from an alcove. He tipped his hat at her.

"In here, in case they have the police after you."

She wasn't mad, just a little flushed and out of breath. She ducked into the doorway and he closed it behind her.

"You skinned your knee."

"I did?" She looked down. "Oh. Yes, I did."

He handed her a handkerchief and she pressed it against her knee.

"And my wallet?"

He handed that over too, and she checked it.

"I didn't steal anything."

"No, I don't suppose you would. Did I pass?"

"Pretty close. A pro would have been able to walk out the front door with a wave goodbye from the waiter."

"I have one more day of training."

"We have too much to cover. You ready? I don't think the police are out there."

"After you. Lead the way, Coach."

"Quite."

8

The shop window, angled at forty-five degrees from the pavement, gave Aubrey an excellent view of the street behind her. There were elegant ladies' shoes on display in the window. Normally, Aubrey would have ogled all of them and then entered the store for a purchase. But in this case, she was searching the glass, looking for him. Hewitt Purnsley of His Majesty's Secret Intelligence Service. He was out there somewhere. Watching her. Following her.

It was early morning, and the street was alive with activity. After a few additional minor exercises in counter-surveillance the night before, Hewitt had seen her to her hotel. It had been a long day and she was fatigued, but she'd found it difficult at first to go to sleep. Her mind swirled with possibilities. She had been switched on, as Hewitt called it. An inner awareness of everything around her was growing, and she was overwhelmed by it.

And it wasn't just the memorizing of license plate numbers, something she was getting good at by the end of that first day, but the whole idea of it, of playing at spying.

"No," she scolded herself again. "Stop calling it that. And certainly, don't call it that in front of Mr. Purnsley." He might get on the transatlantic phone to

John Walton and have her pulled from this assignment.

No, she was going into a foreign, hostile land, intent on engaging in espionage. There was no playing about it. If that attitude crept in one iota during her stay in Nazi Germany, it might very well mean the end of her. The Germans had tried to kill her once already.

She was up with the dawn, bathed and dressed before the city started to come alive. She could see the upper half of the Eiffel Tower from the slim window in her modest hotel room. She could smell the smells and hear the sounds of a city coming alive.

Hewitt was in the lobby, looking like he hadn't even gone to bed. She had no idea where he was staying, whether he too was in a hotel or whether he had a flat. She knew better, now, than to ask these questions outright. Even if he did answer her, they would probably be all lies. Knowing that gave her some confidence. The man sent to train her for her first mission was a professional. She had no way of knowing whether he was the best or not, but she would wager money he was very, very good.

They'd gone over what they'd discussed the day before and discussed the practical exercises, and then she was off. Her assignment: to move about the city and "lose him." He was going to tail her, at first openly, then more discreetly. She was to lose him without seeming to lose him.

He had explained more than once in the short time they'd been together that she was not to let surveillance know she was on to them. To run away, make a mad dash from a tail in a hostile land, was the worst thing she could do. It would confirm their suspicions that she was up to something. And it would only lead to her arrest. It would give them grounds to pick her up and start extracting information from her. She didn't need to be a grizzled grunt of the intelligence world to know that meant torture. She shuddered at the thought. She suspected that the Gestapo, the German secret police, had very effective means of extracting information.

She started off simply enough, trying to catch a glimpse of him without turning around. Once, she turned one hundred and eighty degrees and marched off in the direction she'd just come like she'd forgotten something or changed her mind about something she'd seen in a store window. The first time she pulled that sudden move, she'd caught a glimpse of Hewitt behind her, a half block away. He didn't seem to notice her at all and was doing his own pantomime of window shopping. Then afterwards, when she did the same quick one-eighty again, Hewitt seemed to vanish at will. He was there and then he wasn't.

After a while, she caught glimpses of him again in store windows or the rear glass of taxicabs.

She went into a dress shop, lingered and saw him. The shop's window had its venetian blinds drawn down halfway to block the sun. She could see the lower half of him across the street. The bored-looking shop girls snapped to attention when she spoke to them in French. They'd assumed she was a tourist, but now they gave her some serious attention. It was all for show; in reality she was determining where the rear exit was.

She rebuffed the girls. They took up new customers. Aubrey made her way to the back. When none of the employees were looking, she dashed down the hallway and ran out the back door. She found herself in a narrow passageway that zig-zagged between buildings. She ran past a couple of passed-out drunks, stepping over their scabby ankles and pools of vomit. She finally emerged onto the street that ran parallel to the one she'd just been on.

She looked left and right, but Hewitt Purnsley was nowhere to be seen. She headed off to the Arc de Triomphe. Before the exercise began, Purnsley had designated that famous spot as her rendezvous. Her goal was to make it there without her SIS coach trailing her. She couldn't help but smile. Here she was, two blocks from the Arc, and Hewitt was nowhere in sight. She picked up the pace, glancing only occasionally in windows to try and spot him. She could see the bulk of the Arc in the distance, hear the roar of traffic that ran around it. If she was good, maybe he'd give her a bit of time to herself and she could do some real shopping.

Then she spotted him. Her heart sank. She'd just rounded a corner; the Arc was in full view, two hundred yards away. But there was no mistaking it: he was behind her. He caught up with her just as she reached the monument to the unknown soldier.

"You're one cool customer," she told him grudgingly. "How did you do it?"

"Practice. Going into the store was a bad move. I watched you look at dresses and then move to the rear; knew what you were up to. Running out the back was a dead giveaway to me that my surveillance was blown. Try that trick in Berlin and you'll wind up in 1195 Prinz-Albrecht-Strasse. The basement of Gestapo headquarters."

Aubrey looked dejected.

"There is an art to this. Listen, try and put a crowd between yourself and the tail. Bog them down. Then, at the last moment, hop into a taxi or, better yet, a crowded streetcar that is just pulling away. If you cannot lose a tail, then the meet or drop should be aborted. No question. That's why you always have multiple rendezvous times and places. If you rush this sort of thing, you'll only louse it up, and it'll be your neck.

"You're good, Aubrey. You have some natural instinct. I only wish we had more time for training. But now, I'm afraid we have to start talking about the actual mission."

"I've been briefed."

"Things have changed. There's an added task we'll need you to perform. Come along. I'll tell you all about it."

9

They found a quiet spot in a parkette in the Latin quarter. They took a bench; the only other person was an old man across the way feeding pigeons.

"There is an agent in place, within the Nazi apparatus. It is urgent that you make contact with him. He has information that is vital to peace in Europe."

"How will I—"

"Please, just listen. He will approach you at the exhibition. Here are the challenge-and-response phrases. I need you to memorize them now."

She read the note, committed the words to memory. Two sets of phrases, impossible for anyone to guess.

"Remember, he will approach you and give the challenge. You take it from there."

"Who is he?"

"I can't say. I don't want you going into Germany with that knowledge in your head."

"I see." She handed the note back. He set fire to it with a lighter and it vaporized instantly.

"Nitrocellulose. Flash paper, the kind magicians use," Hewitt said, noting her look of surprise. "My grandfather was a magician."

Aubrey said nothing, just filed this little tidbit about Mr. Purnsley away. It was the first inkling of his true personality that he'd offered. Or had it been a slip?

"Just remember: do not use a phrase before spoken to. Is that understood? There's no guessing in this."

"Yes, you already said that."

"If they're on to Starlight and then extract that info and send someone in as a false flag, they'll have you as a spy too."

"Starlight?"

"Code name for our man on the inside."

"And if no one comes up to me and whispers in my ear?"

"Then you attend the exhibition, learn what you can and leave as planned. Here." He handed her a silver compact. "Let me have the one you have."

She retrieved her own compact from her purse and handed it over.

"This way, I know you won't have the wrong one on you. That one I just gave you has a false bottom. Starlight will give you something to bring back. Slip the note in there. It should fit. He hands you the note; you retire to the ladies' and put it into the compact. I'm telling you this so you'll take it seriously. Never forget how dangerous the package you're carrying is. Once you have it, then comes the tough part."

"Escaping?"

"Negative. You carry on. Put on a brave face, smile, make small talk with the dignitaries and other exhibition attendees. You'll go to dinner with them, out for drinks if they want. Anything but run out of there. That's where character comes into play. I know you have it. You've done things I wouldn't dare try in a million years."

"You flatter me, Mr. Purnsley."

That seemed to set him straight, and he stiffened up. "Just make sure you get the package across the border after the exhibition. No hanging about. You're going to be tailed—just assume it."

"Why's that? I'm just going in as a journalist."

"A journalist is perfect cover for a spy. We use them, but so do the opposition. The Gestapo and Abwehr have plenty of people to keep you under close watch. They've torn the rule book up when it comes to civilized behaviour. Never forget that for a second, no matter how charming they might appear."

"I won't. I've already been on the receiving end of their anger. Saw a man get shot for it." She shuddered inwardly.

"I know. Now, one last meal and then you'll be on your way. My shout."

They did enjoy one last meal together, and this time there was no monkey business. It was just small talk and comments on the wonderful French cuisine. At first, Aubrey was alert to any of Purnsley's espionage tricks. She kept her purse close at hand and protected it anytime a waiter or busboy came by. Purnsley picked up on this and put his hands up.

"We're off duty."

"Are we—I mean you... Are you ever off duty, really?"

"No, never. But I'll suspend training for the evening. Besides, what's the point. You're either ready to fly solo or you aren't."

"And if I'm not, it's curtains for me."

"Possibly. Listen, don't worry. It'll go off without a hitch."

Aubrey nodded, then hesitated for a moment before speaking again. "Hewitt, when that man I took out of Germany was dying in that field, he said something to me."

"I think I remember you telling me something."

"He said that Lazarus must get out. Does that mean anything to you?"

Purnsley sipped his wine.

"Hew?"

"Don't call me that. My sister calls me that. Little Huey. I hate the name."

"Okay, Hewitt. Lazarus—ring a bell?"

"He's a scientist, I believe. Brilliant. They're starting to flee Germany in droves. Someone called it a brain drain in the paper the other day. Seems appropriate."

"Why wouldn't Germany, Hitler, want to keep these brilliant minds in the country?"

"Because most of them are Jews. Either that or they're Reds. This Lazarus does something with molecules, some sort of physics. I was never one for hard science."

"Me neither, except when it came to flying, of course."

"What goes up must come down, that sort of thing?"

She smiled. "So, what about him? Can he be gotten out?"

"Doubtful. If he can, he'll have to do it on his own."

"What about picking him up, like I did with the other guy? I could fly in…"

"Nonsense. Besides, that was all arranged. That was one of ours. We were in contact with him. Do you think he could have evaded the Gestapo without having sufficient training?"

"But they were on to him—they shot at us. Was he betrayed?"

"Probably. We'll never know. Anyway, enough about this Lazarus. Just concentrate on the job at hand. Your train leaves in two hours."

Aubrey was booked on the overnight to Berlin. The trip would take eight hours. They finished their meal, and Hewitt Purnsley said his goodbyes as he hailed a taxi for her. Aubrey thought he would return with her to the hotel but evidently, he wanted to make a clean break right there. She took no offense.

She had not fully unpacked for her short stay in Paris. As she put the few things back into her suitcase, she noticed something at the bottom of it. Something she had forgotten she had. She pulled the Colt .45 out of her bag and held it in her hands. It had been a last-minute decision, nicking her father's pistol. She had decided it was the only way she would have peace of mind, knowing that her father didn't have access to a loaded handgun. She stared at it speculatively. Or had there been another reason?

She was, after all, going into hostile territory. Had she felt some subconscious need to take it? She hadn't mentioned it to Hewitt. Although they'd only spent two days together, she could tell what his reaction would be. He would have called her a damn fool for trying to bring a weapon into the Reich. He might have even confiscated it, or, worse, called the whole thing off.

She didn't even have a holster for it. Only her tan flying coat had pockets big enough for it. She could hardly wear that to an elegant ball. But then again, what need would she have to bring a loaded pistol to an elegant fancy-dress ball? The pistol went back into the bag, stuffed down into the bottom.

The compact Hewitt had given her was packed last, after she'd sat down on the bed and fiddled with it for a while. The false bottom was hard to undo but eventually, by sticking her thumbnail in it, she got it open. She practised it a few more times; the last thing she wanted to do was be caught fiddling with it in the washroom of the Air Ministry of Nazi Germany.

She boarded the train to Berlin and a fat man in a wrinkled grey suit shifted his seat to allow her a window view. She thanked him, speaking in what little German she had. She'd taken it at Rockingham Girls' Collegiate. She'd had no need of the French classes, of course; she spoke that better than the instructor.

She gazed out at the busy platform in Paris and noticed Hewitt Purnsley standing a hundred feet back from the train, hands in the pockets of his trench coat. For a moment they locked eyes. Then the train hooted and started to chug forward. Hewitt faded into the crowd and was gone.

As the train rolled across the French countryside, falling asleep proved an impossible task at first. Finally, the rhythmic clicking of the wheels over the tracks lulled her and she dreamt of Michigan and Ferguson and her father. The dream was abruptly ended by the slamming open of the compartment doors. A thin man no older than she was entered, carrying two battered suitcases. He was wearing a faded grey suit two sizes too large for him. The suitcases went on the rack over his head and he plunked down opposite her. The man who'd given up his seat had been awakened by the newcomer as well. Aubrey saw him cast a disapproving eye at the young man.

The thin man unwrapped something strong-smelling from some waxed paper and the compartment was instantly filled with the odour. The man looked sheepishly up at Aubrey from his meal and offered it across to her. It looked like pâté. Her stomach grumbled; she was tempted to try it, but shook her head and smiled at the man. He was charming; his smile back showed a mouthful of pearly white teeth, and he had an infectious grin. There was a mole on his cheek below his right eye, and his hair, tucked up under a cap, looked very dark and oily. The man offered the delicacy to the German man, who ruffled his newspaper and held it higher to rebuff the offer. Aubrey changed her mind; she reached her hand out and snatched a small bit of beef pâté on a cracker. That delighted the newcomer to no end. She thanked him in English.

"You're American?" he asked.

"I am. How can you tell?"

"I know many Americans. You have come to my country in droves, it appears, after the war." The man wolfed down two crackers and continued speaking. A small dab of pâté bobbed at the corner of his mouth. He then opened a bottle of wine and procured two glasses. He filled them both and offered one across to Aubrey. She took it gratefully.

"You're spoiling me, sir."

"My name is Frederick. Frederick Oppenheim," the man said, and with that name came a snort of derision from the other man, who ruffled his papers again. Frederick looked at the man and then at Aubrey and winked.

"Where did you learn English so well, Frederick?"

"In school, all German children are taught many languages. English is the most popular and probably the most useful for the years to come."

"Why is that?"

"All part of the master plan, our dear leader's plans for world conquest." He tilted his head forward and winked again. Despite his attempts at whispering, the man across from him heard what was said and lowered his paper shield.

"You should learn to watch your mouth, young man."

"We're still in France: *'Liberté, Egalité, Fraternité.'*"

"Yes, you idiot, but if you haven't noticed, we're travelling eastward." The newspaper went back up.

More pâté was offered, and this time Aubrey nodded at the dab on his mouth.

"My apologies," he said, hastily applying his handkerchief to it. "I haven't dined with a lady in a while."

"Why were you in France?"

"I was attempting at getting a permit to travel to England. I have relatives there."

"Oh, I see. No luck?"

"The permit has been filed. It will take them several weeks to reject it," Frederick said, and laughed. "Such is life. I'm just glad I'll be around to see our dear leader's great plans for the Fatherland come true." His voice rose as he said it, and he turned to the man with the papers. There was just a snort and more ruffling.

Despite Frederick's optimism, the man with the newspapers was telling the truth. They were headed east, to the German border at Alsace. Even Aubrey, an outsider, felt uncomfortable about the young man's politicized comments.

It was dawn when the train stopped on the French side of the border. A French administrative official boarded, accompanied by two unshaven soldiers with rifles over their shoulders. They went from car to car, compartment to compartment. They weren't checking anything, not even tickets. It was unclear what they were looking for.

The door to their compartment slid open and the official stepped in; the two soldiers stood behind him in the doorway. Frederick had stowed what was left of his meal, and the half-empty wine bottle was tucked back into his jacket. He sat upright and forward on his seat and looked right at the French official with proud but pleading eyes. The official gave him the once-over, barely looked at Aubrey, and ignored the fellow with the newspapers. Seemingly satisfied, he turned and marched away down the corridor. One of the soldiers caught Aubrey's eye and grinned, but there was a call for him to come and he scooted away, leaving the compartment door open.

After another ten-minute wait at the station, Aubrey finally saw the official and the two soldiers escorting someone off the train.

"What is happening there, Frederick?"

"An escaped convict? Maybe he was escaping from a trip to Devil's Island."

"The island off South America? I read about that. Does Germany have overseas prisons?"

"No, we've created several homegrown nightmares within our own borders. Maybe one day our dear leader will export this invention."

"Let's hope not." Aubrey knew she shouldn't respond to these provocative statements, but somehow, she couldn't help it.

The train started up again and moved deeper into the Vosges Mountains just as dawn was breaking. Aubrey stared out the window and spontaneously, automatically, began plotting a course through the peaks—what altitude she would fly, how long it would take her. She wanted to keep her skills sharp.

Then they were on the other side and the Tricolour was replaced by flapping swastikas by the dozen. At least twenty of them for every French flag she'd seen. There was no denying it: she had crossed into the Reich.

"Ahh, home," Frederick said. The news junkie chuckled, then tucked the paper away and produced his passport. Aubrey and Frederick did likewise, and with a start Aubrey saw that her generous young German friend had additional papers to carry. She saw the corner of a yellow six-pointed star at the top of one of them, tucked in his passport. She saw that the man next to her had noticed it too.

The train stopped and there were shouts outside, and then they heard the clomp of boots—heavy ones, that could only be military issue—come down the middle of the carriage. The banging open of compartment doors grew louder. Moments later, the door on their compartment was flung open. An official in a black uniform with a swastika armband stepped inside. Behind her she saw German soldiers: fresh faced, clean shaven and utterly terrifying. They had rifles too, but they were carried upright over their shoulders, whereas the French soldiers had carried theirs sloppily. The rifle straps were polished and pulled tight. The man with the armband seemed to gleam, too; everything that was black and leather shone like glass.

He did not yell, as Aubrey had half-expected, but rather asked for papers in a calm voice, a sinister smile at his mouth. Aubrey held hers up and he took it first.

"Ahh, American," he said in English not half as good as Frederick's.

"Yes, journalist. Here for the air exhibition."

"I see. The Reich welcomes journalists. We just hope you'll report what you've seen truthfully."

Aubrey was about to question whether a border official could make such a statement, but bit her tongue.

The official wrote something in her passport and handed it back. His joviality vanished as he turned his attention to Frederick. The young man handed his credentials over; they were leafed through quickly.

"You must come with us."

"Why's that?" Aubrey said, and Frederick turned on her. His civility had vanished, but it was out of concern.

"Miss Aubrey, please, don't."

"He's right, miss," said the official. "Do not concern yourself with our affairs. You, up!" he shouted. Frederick grabbed his shabby suitcases off the rack and was led out. There was no time for him to turn and say goodbye. The two guards had their arms around him. In a second, he was gone.

"Why'd they do that? Was he in the wrong compartment?" she asked the man next to her after the soldiers had left.

"He is not permitted to ride first class in German trains whilst within the Reich's borders."

"And why's that?"

"Because he's a Jew, and it's the law. Take your young friend's advice, miss. Do not get involved. You can only get hurt and hurt those around you."

"A lot of good you did, and you're a fellow German."

"Yes, and I've learned to keep my mouth shut. Your friend should have learned that as well. Maybe they will teach him. They have a place for people like him." He gave an icy smile.

"One of those camps he mentioned?"

"Yes. It's called Dachau."

10

Aubrey checked into the Hotel Adlon on the Unter Den Linden. Her room had a commanding view of the Brandenburg Gates. She'd seen that famous portal once before, from the air, on her way across Europe in the 1934 air rally when she'd flown over the German capital. What had been lost on her from that first viewing, and which assaulted her eyes now, were the flags and bunting. The entire Pariser Platz seemed to be decorated in red, white and black swastikas. Large banners were strung from the roofs to street level on every building, including the hotel. She could hear them fluttering outside her room. The sight of all those twisted crosses, those wretched claws—no, she realized. Gears. That's what they reminded her of: the swastikas looked like gears in a machine. Maybe that was intentional—the machine being the state, its gears turning ruthlessly, ready to maim anyone who opposed it.

She thought of poor Frederick, hauled from the train. Had he merely been kicked off for the offense of riding in first class, or had he been arrested? Was he on his way to Dachau this very moment? She shuddered. He'd seemed like an outspoken but harmless young man.

She reminded herself that she had a job to do. No, a mission: that's what Hewitt Purnsley had called it. She wondered what the confident Englishman was up to at this moment. Perhaps sitting next to a wireless, waiting for radio reports of the apprehension of a female American spy? There was no way of contacting him. The plan was for her to depart Germany in three days, after the exhibition ended, and make her way to Paris. She had the return ticket and a room booked in the same Parisian hotel. She would have to wait for him to make contact.

Three days here… She wondered if she would go colour blind from all the black, red and white flags, or would she become accustomed to them? Would they cease to assault her senses? She couldn't fathom that possibility.

Suddenly, she realized she was exhausted. Robbed of sleep on the train, she looked longingly at the single bed in her hotel room. But first things first. She dumped the contents of her bag out onto the bed. The black automatic pistol fell out last and she scooped it up, then tucked it back into the bag until she figured out what to do with it. Her clothes went into the dresser, and her more formal outfits went into a little alcove with hangers. John Walton's girl had done a good job with shopping; the two outfits she'd purchased for Aubrey would do nicely. Certainly, the shops in Sacred never carried such haute couture. She only wished she'd had time in Paris to do some shopping herself.

There was a knock on the door. The open bag was still on her bed. One would have to deliberately look in it to spot the pistol, but…

Another knock.

"Fraulein Endeavours," someone on the other side called in English.

"One moment, *bitte*," she replied.

She pulled the pistol from the bag, lifted the mattress and shoved the pistol under it. That would do for now. She stepped over to the door and pulled it open.

Outside were two men dressed in the blue uniforms of the Luftwaffe. One was a corporal, the other a private. She sighed quietly with relief; she had half-expected Nazis in their evil black uniforms to be standing there, or men from the Gestapo in their raincoats and fedoras.

She greeted the men warmly and invited them in, but they declined. The corporal informed her that they were there to escort her to the exhibition. They'd been informed of her arrival.

Really? she thought. That was quick. Either the hotel had called it in, or perhaps they'd been waiting in a car and had seen her arrive. Very efficient. And disturbing. She begged five more minutes to freshen up, and then hurried down and met them in the lobby.

The men led her outside to a Ford Rheinlander, which was parked in front of the hotel. The two of them climbed in the front, which left the mohair-covered rear seat entirely to her. Aubrey sat back and watched the Berlin city centre, the Mitte district, whiz by. The airman drove; the corporal turned around to talk.

"We're in the Luftwaffe," he said.

"I gathered that from your uniforms. There are a lot of uniforms in Germany."

"Oh, yes. More so every day. Military service is now compulsory. Thank you for coming, Fraulein

Endeavours. That is an unusual name, by the way. Is it common in America?"

"No, I don't think so. There was a Captain Endeavours in the Revolutionary War, but we could never establish the relation."

"Your fight against the British—you were successful. We were not so fortunate," the corporal said, and laughed.

"You guys seem more relaxed than the others I've met. One of them was dressed in black."

The smiles fell away from both men's faces.

"*Schutzstaffel*," the corporal said. "The SS. They are dangerous, Miss Endeavours."

"Call me Aubrey."

"Aubrey—that is a nice name, too."

"Why are they so crotchety?" Aubrey asked.

"The SS? I don't know what 'crotchety' means, but I can guess. Why are they that way? Because they are in charge."

Aubrey smiled grimly. "Where are you taking me?"

"Southwest of the city, to Adlershof Airfield. That is where the exhibition is being held. Germany is eager to export its latest aeronautical achievements to the rest of the world. There will be buyers there from all over: Japan, Greece, South America. And of course, journalists like yourself."

"Why am I getting the special treatment, a personal car sent just for me?"

"Because, Miss Endeavours, you are a famous pilot from America. We are honoured to have you in Germany, and Hans and I are even more honoured to be driving you."

"Why, thank you, gents. I think we're going to get along just swell."

"There will be plenty of sightseeing opportunities for the delegates and journalists. We want to show Germany off to the world. And next year, we have the Olympics."

The car paused at the main entrance to the Adlershof airfield. There were more armed soldiers; none of them seemed as friendly as the corporal and Hans. Identification was checked and orders were barked. The two airmen brought the car over to a large tent just inside the main gate.

"This is the check-in, Aubrey. You have press credentials?"

"I do. What's the deal?"

"You'll get in that line and be processed; we'll meet up with you on the other side."

"See you then."

There were thirty people in line, all men. A couple of them noticed a woman joining their ranks and turned curiously. Most had scowls on their faces. The man who got in line immediately behind her was the only one who offered a smile.

"Forgive my colleagues, miss," he said. "They spend so much time hunched over a typewriter they rarely get to see a pretty face."

"I don't think that's it. They don't get to see a woman's face, pretty or otherwise, in their line of work."

"True." He stuck out a hand. "I am Richard Fuchs. I am a journalist with the *Berliner Morgenpost*."

She shook hands with him. "Aubrey Endeavours, freelance writer. Here to write a few articles for some magazines."

"*Time Magazine?*"

"Gosh, no."

"But they should put your pretty picture on the cover."

Little did this fellow know that she'd already graced the cover of *Time* after the Pulitzer race. There was a roar overhead as seven aircraft in an inverted V flew over the aerodrome.

"Wow, fantastic!" Aubrey said.

The sound of the seven fighters roaring overhead, even at a thousand feet, was deafening. The formation banked to the east and was lost from sight. The check-in line moved forward. The men around her were jabbering in all manner of languages. She picked out the odd French phrase here and there, and some Italian. No English, though.

A desk in front of her became free and Aubrey stepped forward and put on her best smile. A pimply-faced corporal checked her papers and smiled back. He was about to stamp them when an officer wearing one of those dreaded black uniforms stepped behind him and grabbed her credentials out of his hand. He was young, somewhat handsome. She could see a wisp of blonde hair up under his cap—a cap adorned with the death's head logo. He had lightning bolts on one side of his collar, and on his sleeve was a diamond patch with *SD* inside of it, indicating the *Sicherheitsdienst*—the Nazi intelligence agency.

"Your papers are not in order," he said in stilted yet crisp English.

"How can that be? They were just issued."

"These forms are no longer accepted."

"I don't understand."

Richard Fuchs was all checked in and had his pass in his hand. He came over to assist.

"What seems to be the problem?"

"Are you colleagues?" the Nazi asked.

"Yes."

"Do you work for the same organization?"

"No. I'm German. This is an American guest in our country Herr *Hauptsturmführer*—Captain."

"That has no bearing. Our embassy in the United States made an error. They used the wrong form. We no longer accept this."

"As of when?" Richard asked. Aubrey saw a fire start to burn in the SS officer's eyes.

"As of last week. New forms have been issued."

"I was in the middle of the Atlantic last week," Aubrey said. "How would I know?"

"It makes no difference, Miss Endeavours. You will have to return to your embassy here in Berlin. Perhaps they can assist you in obtaining the correct press credentials."

"Endeavours?" a man in a dark suit said. He had been standing off to the right of the discussion, talking with some high-ranking Luftwaffe officers. Being that he was on the other side of the tables, Aubrey assumed he was involved in running the exhibition.

The SS officer turned and saw who'd shown an interest in the American's dilemma. He became ramrod straight and clicked the heels of his shin-high leather boots together smartly.

"Count von Villiez. I had no idea you were there."

The man ignored the SS officer and gazed at Aubrey. He had a head of glistening, slicked-back, black hair and piercing blue eyes. His jaw was square and strong, and his upper torso spread out wide and was covered by a very well-tailored suit. She noticed several gold rings and a gold-embossed badge on his lapel with the German cross on it.

"You are Aubrey Endeavours, the American pilot?"

"Yes."

Finally, the count turned his attention to the SS man, who was still at attention. "This lady is my personal guest to the exhibition. If I do not find that she has been treated with the utmost respect and consideration, I will speak to Herr Reichsmarschall Goering personally. Perhaps even the Führer."

"Yes, Herr—Count von Villiez," the Nazi officer said, and again he clicked his heels.

Aubrey saw that Richard had passed through the turnstile into the exhibition after someone of obvious power had come to her defence. Good thing, too. The SS officer looked ready to explode.

Aubrey extended her hand to her new benefactor, expecting this handsome devil to shake it. He lifted it gently and kissed it.

"Oh my." She felt her face grow hot.

"Miss Endeavours, I was delighted to learn you would be attending our exhibition. I trust the men I sent to fetch you from your hotel were courteous?"

"You sent them? Yes, they were. But how did you know where I was staying?"

A mischievous grin came across the count's lips. "I have connections with the government. Your application for press credentials listed the hotel. Do you not remember putting that down?"

Of course she didn't. She'd never filled them out. John Walton had had someone do it. They had been handed to her as she was boarding the steamer for France.

"Yes, of course. My apologies. I am just a little fatigued from the journey, I guess."

"When did you land?"

"Three days ago," Aubrey said. Great, kid, she thought. You just admitted you've been in Europe three days.

The count chuckled. "Long voyages affect people in different ways. Regardless, we are most eager to have you here. Your exploits are well known." He turned back to the young man in the sinister black uniform. "The captain here has made a mistake, and we will overlook this slight incongruity in your paperwork. Isn't that right, Herr Hauptsturmführer?"

"*Ja wohl*, Count von Villiez."

The SS captain shouted at the corporal behind the desk, who in turn stamped the press credentials and handed Aubrey a cardboard placard on a lanyard.

The count shook his head. "You will not need to wear that ugly thing around your neck, Mademoiselle." He turned to the captain once more. "This woman has my personal pass. Is that clear?" The men nodded almost as one. "Good. Please spread the word to your colleagues in the SS."

Aubrey watched the young officer's face; he had taken about as much humiliation as he could endure from this non-uniformed man, no matter how well-connected he might be. He was just regaining himself and straightening his tunic when the count took Aubrey's arm and personally escorted her into the exhibition.

"I can't tell you how excited I am to have you here. You're working as a journalist?"

The way the count said it made her think maybe he was hinting that her job as a journalist was just a cover.

"Yes, just started. Freelance. Aviation articles."

"A young girl like you with your skills, your bravery, should be up there amongst the clouds."

"That's the plan. But first I need to make some money writing articles and buy a plane."

"Wonderful. Maybe you'll buy a German plane?"

"Maybe a Bf 109." She grinned at him.

"Why not? We will start exporting them eventually. I can think of no better ambassador in the United States than Aubrey Endeavours, world-famous aviatrix."

"You are laying it on a bit thick, Count."

"Please call me Helmut. Yes, I do tend to do that. In my line of work, I do not get to interact very much with pretty ladies. You are reaping the benefits."

"And what line of work might that be? Forgive me for being rude, but I don't know who you are."

His laugh was a pleasant baritone. "Of course, I don't expect you to know who I am." He stopped, dropped her arm and bowed quickly. "I am Count Helmut von Villiez, the eighth baron of Upper Bavaria."

"Royalty?"

He laughed again. "At one time I would have been called an aristocrat. I'm afraid royalty in my country now wears a black uniform."

"You're not in the military?"

"No, my family is in aviation. We make many of the components that go into German aircraft production." He swept his arm around the exhibition. There were a dozen hangars, all of them with various planes poking their propellors out and hundreds of people gathered around all of them. "And as you can see, business is very good these days."

"I see. You're an industrialist."

"An ugly word. I prefer inventor, or perhaps entrepreneur. That's a French word. Do you know what that means?"

"I speak French."

"Ahh, yes. I remember reading that."

"What else have you read?"

"That you are fearless. That you flew and beat most of the men in your country at their own game. We Germans like a strong, resourceful woman. Listen, Miss Endeavours—"

"Please, it's Aubrey. After what you did for me back there with the captain, we're practically pals."

"All right—Aubrey it is. Now, I have to attend to an important business meeting. You have the run of the place, see what you like, but promise me we can resume this conversation later today?"

"I don't see why not. Where will I find you?"

"Don't worry, I will find you. Enjoy yourself."

She watched him walk off, then turned her attention to the exhibition. Richard Fuchs emerged from the crowd of journalists and convention-goers and sidled up to her. He gave her an odd look.

"Just who are you, exactly?"

"*Time*'s cover girl of the week, March 25th, 1929." That stopped him in his tracks. She toddled off. He recovered himself and came up next to her again as she headed to a group of static display aircraft.

"No, seriously."

"I did some flying back home, won some awards. Got some press. I flew in the air rally last year, the Challenge International. I was forced down. Engine trouble."

"Oh, right—I think I remember that. Your picture was in my paper. I knew I had seen you somewhere before. I wish I had a copy of it; I would get your autograph."

"Maybe some other time."

"Look, there are some colleagues of mine clustered over there, pretending they know what they're looking at. I should rejoin them. Do you mind if we meet up later?"

"The count beat you to it, I'm afraid. But maybe you could come along too?"

"Doubtful," he said, looking crestfallen. "The count won't have time for a mid-level journalist like me. Plus, three wheels makes a tipsy cart."

"Is that 'three's a crowd' in German?"

"Precisely. What hotel are you staying at?"

"You move fast."

Richard Fuchs grinned. "No time like the present—isn't that what you Americans say?"

"Sure. I'm at the Adlon."

Fuchs gave her a last dazzling smile, then crossed the tarmac and was greeted heartily by some men in long trench coats and thick spectacles.

Aubrey looked around her, not sure where to start. The scope and scale of the air base were daunting. She couldn't remember any airfield back home being this big. They were mostly just grass airstrips with rather frazzled-looking wind direction balloons hanging from poles. Despite the size of the airfield, she knew she was home: it had the same sounds and smells she loved so much. Engines revving up, getting ready for takeoff or feathering down to a landing. The smell of grease and aviation fuel drifted past her nose.

She shielded her eyes and watched as, one by one, the fighters from that impressive inverted wing formation started to come in. The hangar nearest to her held one of them on static display. Smooth, rivet-less sides. Menacing machine guns poking out all over the place. She wandered over to it. A man in a Luftwaffe uniform was talking to a crowd of a dozen men, most of them in uniforms themselves, the flags of their countries on their shoulders: Italy, Poland, some she didn't recognize. She joined the back of the crowd and pretended to listen, but instead she studied the plane. Its configuration was familiar... Then it hit her. This was one of the buggers that had tried to stitch her up over the German countryside.

It was an impressive plane, the last of the biplanes. A Heinkel 51, the placard in front of it said. The officer stopped talking and the crowd of onlookers and prospective buyers dispersed around the aircraft or moved off to others. Aubrey went up to the machine, grabbed hold of one of the struts supporting the wings and pulled on it.

"Very solid," she said.

The men around her either didn't notice her or didn't care. A Japanese man with a camera seemed annoyed that he couldn't get a clear shot without her in it. He bowed several times and then made a sweeping motion with his hand.

"Thing of beauty, isn't it?" she said. "Deadly beauty." The Japanese man started clicking his camera and ignored her. "Well, pardon me all over the place."

Aubrey busied herself for the rest of the day checking out the planes. There were sales presentations by pilots, technical personnel and representatives from the manufacturers, all extolling the virtues of German aeronautics.

Several of the attendees asked specific questions about ceiling limits, stall rates, fuel consumption. For the older planes this information was given up freely. It was only when she attended a presentation on the Bf 109 that she heard the word 'classified.' It was always said with the proverbial wink and grin, and the asker of the question always went away satisfied.

The one example of the Bf 109 on static display was kept well back from the crowds. It was cordoned off with thick velvet rope befitting the king of the air. Aubrey found the aircraft beautiful and menacing. There were a half dozen soldiers standing between the gawkers and the plane. It was brand new, one of the first prototypes; the others were at high-security bases, she knew, undergoing trials. Messerschmitt, the manufacturer of the plane, had representatives there to answer questions. They were hopeful the new plane would be selected as the primary fighter of the Luftwaffe.

Aubrey studied the graceful hunter from thirty feet away and could find no faults. It was perfection in stressed aluminum, with its framed glass canopy and inverted twelve cylinders. Its lines reminded her of a shark. The black muzzles of weaponry protruded from its snout, and the exhaust pipes vented back along the fuselage.

She was staring at the future of aviation, and despite this being the weapon of a belligerent nation, the Third Reich, she found it thrilling.

"A marvellous achievement, isn't it?" said a voice at her side. It was the count; he had come up behind her, and she felt a giddy sensation in her stomach akin to putting an airplane into a steep dive. That burring sensation in her gut she'd come to love so much.

"She looks fast."

"She is. And deadly. Twin standard 7.62 machine guns. They want to put a twenty-millimetre cannon on it."

"Should you be telling me this?"

"We have not hidden this. We are showing this plane to the world. We already have orders coming in from countries that want to purchase it—Spain, Finland. Perhaps even you Americans would be interested in purchasing it. I know that your air force is seriously behind in preparations."

"Preparations for what?"

"For the future," the count said, and smiled.

Aubrey knew what he meant. Her uncle had mentioned the inevitable war that was looming on the horizon. Nazi Germany was indeed belligerent. Hitler certainly was, and with a man like that in total control of a nation, war was a foregone conclusion.

"This is a two-seat model?" Aubrey asked.

"Yes, it's a trainer. Would you like to go up in it?"

Her eyes widened. "Very much so."

"I can arrange it. I can take you up personally."

"What a thrill!"

"Aubrey, there is a reception tonight at my home. A small gathering. I would very much like you to attend."

"Oh… I don't know."

"Say yes. It may be your only chance to meet Herr Reichsmarschall Goering. He is honouring me with his presence, and I know he would very much like to meet you."

"I wouldn't know how to talk or act at an event like that," she said, flustered. "I'm just a country bumpkin. I'd end up embarrassing you, ruining your event. Probably not a good idea."

"You are a famous aviatrix from America. He would love to bore you with his war stories. Please come to my home. It is not far from here. We can leave from the exhibition."

"I'm not dressed."

"Nonsense. You are perfect. I have some business to attend to, so please enjoy the rest of the exhibition and I will collect you closer to three. It's a short drive to my home in Wannsee."

Aubrey remembered the writing on the back of the picture: Lydia Frick, Wannsee.

"If you insist," she said.

"I do," the count said, and smiled.

When Aubrey went to the front gate at three, she spied the count talking to the two young airmen who had driven her to the exhibition. They were ramrod straight and threw up salutes, but the count ignored them. He spotted her emerging from the airfield and waved her over.

Richard Fuchs was there too, with a gaggle of journalists.

"You finished for the day?" she asked him.

"We are. Would you let me show you some of the sights of Berlin? We're headed to a bar."

"Not tonight. I have a date, remember?"

Richard saw who she was talking about. He turned his back on the count. "I cannot compete with that."

"Don't say that. I hardly know him. I hardly know you, for that matter."

"Another time, perhaps. You'll be here tomorrow?"

"Wouldn't miss it."

"Who was that?" the count asked when she joined him.

"A reporter friend of mine. German. Works for one of your newspapers."

"I've never seen him. But then again, reporters buzz around me all day; I don't take the time to get to know them any more than I would a house fly."

"You don't like reporters much, do you?"

"A necessary evil."

"I'm a reporter."

"You're the exception, my dear. I took the liberty of discharging your minders."

"I saw that. They seemed frightened of you."

"Just being good German soldiers."

"I see."

"This way." He led her over to a massive Mercedes Benz touring car. There were side pipes coming out of the engine as thick as those on a warplane.

"Look at this beast," Aubrey said, giving a low whistle.

"Two-ninety horsepower, top speed of one hundred and twenty miles. My driver got it up to that speed once on the new Autobahn. It was thrilling."

"Almost as good as flying one of those 109s."

"Almost."

"You mentioned you would take me up in one."

"All in good time, my dear. All in good time. First, we have to dine and meet the top brass. We can discuss the flight later tonight."

He showed Aubrey into the rear of the big car. There was a thick ruby-coloured curtain hanging in the gap between the driver and the passenger compartment. The count went around the other side and the chauffeur opened the door for him. He slid onto the seat beside Aubrey, the door was slammed shut and they were safely cocooned.

There was a well-stocked bar built into the back of the front seats below the curtain, and he poured her a sweet vermouth.

"This is the only way to travel," Aubrey said, and she sank back into the comfortable seat with her cocktail.

"Is it? said the count. "I wouldn't know."

"You wouldn't know what it was like to drive your own tractor or walk ten miles to town?"

"No, I would not. My family is one of the few aristocratic ones that has not had their family fortunes privatized."

"Who has?"

"Jews, mostly." The way he said 'Jews' was neutral; she could not tell if he despised them or felt sympathy. She decided it was somewhere in between.

With drinks poured, the car motored out onto the Autobahn for the drive to Wannsee. The car rumbled at first, and then the engine smoothed out and grew high in tone as it sped up. Aubrey sipped her vermouth and looked out the window at the passing countryside.

"My word, we are really flying. I wish Father's truck could go this fast. I might give up flying for auto racing."

"Have you been to an auto race? The European Grand Prix is in two weeks."

"I haven't, and sadly, I can't stick around for it."

"That's disappointing. It really is something to see—a real blood sport."

"I know. I've read of the crashes. Drivers killed—spectators, too."

"They know the risks, those racing the cars and those coming to see it."

"Still."

They passed some slower-moving sedans that went by in a whirl.

"How fast are we going?"

"I'd say at least a hundred miles an hour."

"Incredible."

"Another drink?"

"A short one." Aubrey remembered Hewitt Purnsley's cautionary words about getting tipsy. She was already feeling a warm glow from the drink. Hopefully they would have soda water at this shindig she was attending.

The count's house was not what she had been expecting. He read her disappointment.

"You thought I lived in a castle."

"Of course—like Dracula."

He chuckled. "The family had one centuries ago, but the villagers sacked it and set the torch to it. The ruins are still there. Perhaps you are interested?"

"I don't have the time, Count."

"Please, call me Helmut."

"Helmut."

"That's my given name. You can call me Your Grace or Count von Villiez when we are around others. Not for my sake, of course, but to avoid offending anyone who still holds on to these sentimentalities from a bygone era."

"You've moved on."

"We had to. Our positions were abolished in 1918, as part of the German revolution, to keep the allies happy. All we kept were our titles."

"And money."

"Those who saw it coming and turned their lands and holdings into cash deposited into Swiss banks, yes. Most are penniless. I'm somewhere in between."

"Doesn't look like it to me." The house they were approaching was not a Gothic castle, but it was still impressive. She judged it to be around the same size as the east wing of the White House, a place she'd visited personally with some of the other Ninety-Nines, the group of women flyers that Earhart had set up. Helmut's stately house was a pale yellow in colour, with a large circular driveway that led under an overhang.

The driver stopped the car at the front steps and opened the rear doors for Aubrey and the count. There was light chamber music coming from inside the house, and when they stepped inside, Aubrey saw that the foyer was crowded with people, most of them in uniform.

"Your Grace, we started without you," one rather tipsy senior officer said.

"My apologies, Herr General. I was detained at the exhibition." The count nodded at Aubrey. "This young American woman has enthralled me with her stories of derring-do." He clapped his hands for attention. "Gentlemen, allow me to introduce the world-famous aviatrix, Miss Aubrey Endeavours."

The crowd turned to her as one, and Aubrey saw glances of surprise and interest passing amongst many of the party-goers.

Helmut said, "Please, Aubrey, make yourself at home." A waiter in tails came by with a tray of white wine and the count took one and handed it to her.

So much for soda, she thought. There was a bar in one corner. Several officers in grey uniforms, red stripes down their pant legs, were holding it up. They all had gold braid at their epaulettes, medals on their chests, and braided gold ropes under their arms. It looked like the entire senior command of Germany was here.

The wine was ice cold and very dry.

"From my vineyard in southern Germany," the count said, noting her look of approval.

"This is dangerous stuff."

The count took Aubrey around and introduced her to several of the key men in attendance; she was the only woman there. She couldn't remember all their names, and inwardly scolded herself: this was information she knew Hewitt might be interested in. She had somehow managed to work her way into the heart of Germany's military command social circles. Or maybe he had known this would happen.

Several of the Germans turned their noses up at the rather simply dressed and unglamorous American flyer. Some of them turned on the lasciviousness charm, but they only went so far. Maybe they sensed the count had his eyes set on Aubrey, something she was becoming aware of herself.

She decided she would use it to her advantage, but would stop it before it went too far. At least that was what she told herself. She found herself becoming more and more attracted to him. He was striking, handsome, well mannered, and had the gift of the gab as he worked the room with her by his side.

Suddenly, she saw someone she recognized, and fear gripped her stomach. It was the young Nazi captain who had examined her press credentials that morning and found them inadequate. He was standing alone in a corner, sipping a glass of clear liquid, observing. Their eyes met. He set his glass down, strode across to meet them and threw up a knife-handed Nazi salute. Aubrey wasn't sure who he was saluting. The count seemed a little dismayed and only nodded his head in return. A look of shock came over the young captain's face but then quickly disappeared as he turned his attention to Aubrey.

"Miss Endeavours. It is pleasant to see you again so soon."

"Why thank you, Herr…"

"Schmidt. Hauptsturmführer Schmidt. I am attached to Herr Reichsmarschall Goering."

"Is he here?" the count asked.

"The Reichsmarschall is delayed, Your Grace. He will be here momentarily."

"The man likes to make an entrance," Helmut said.

There it was again: that look of shock on the SS officer's face. He was no doubt taking it all in, every little transgression against his masters by this civilian—a titled, noble civilian, but a civilian nonetheless.

Without any further updates and with a total lack of small talk, the SS man went away to speak to some of his comrades. Aubrey caught all of them looking over at her and the count; they were clearly speaking about the two of them. They did not look away quickly when she did catch them; they were the masters here, not her. Not even the count was in charge. She should be the one afraid. And that she was, indeed. The sight of those sinister black uniforms standing before her, speaking to her, speaking *about* her, shook her to her core. They had a much more devastating effect in person. That was by design, she realized.

"What is your connection to all this?" Aubrey asked the count when they had a brief moment to themselves.

"What do you mean?"

"I know you were in the air force during the war. That reporter, Fuchs, told me."

"What else did he tell you?"

"You were an ace, decorated. Why aren't you still in uniform?"

"I was wounded in the war. I am not a hundred percent, and I do not want to pretend that I am still worthy of wearing a uniform of the Reich. It doesn't seem right. My medals are locked away upstairs. My uniform, too. It's in the past."

"But these men defer to you like you were a general. That one certainly does." She nodded at the SS man.

"I have been afforded an honorary rank of colonel, and I have certain pull. My companies are very well known in Germany and I have contributed in my own way to the rebuilding of my country. I have the Führer's blessing, if you will."

"So you weren't lying this morning? You could have spoken to him about me?"

"Yes, if necessary, I would have called him at his estate in Berchtesgaden if I had to, but I knew that was not necessary. That youngster there was just strutting his stuff for show."

"He scares me."

"I'm no great fan of the SS, Aubrey, but the Führer has brought our country back from the brink. No one can deny that."

"I need a drink." So much for the club soda.

The noise of the soiree was growing in intensity. Several more officers arrived and there was a round of "Heil Hitler," and then finally a long entourage of vehicles pulled up to the house. It had grown dark, and their headlights lit up the candlelit room.

Aubrey was feeling no pain by now. She scolded herself internally for not slowing down. There was food, delicious hors d'oeuvres, and she did her best to devour as many as possible while every German officer rushed to the front door to present themselves to the latecomers.

The entourage disgorged its occupants and a troop of black-helmeted men came into the foyer and formed a phalanx. Then up the steps came the most enormous man Aubrey had ever seen, wearing a pale blue uniform adorned with more medals and buttons than she could count. He also wore a maniacal grin that bunched up the jowls of his fat face as he waddled up the stairs. He had a short, gilded staff in one meaty paw, and he raised it in return to the Nazi salutes. Even the count clicked his heels and shot his hand out into the air. The count's servants came to attention, frozen in their tracks. Aubrey was the only one not paying homage to the enormous fellow entering the house. The massive man spied her and made a beeline for her. The count introduced the latecomer to her: Hermann Goering.

11

Aubrey did some sort of American version of a curtsy and immediately felt foolish. Herr Reichsmarschall Goering, Hitler's right-hand man, smiled manically and grasped her hand in both of his pudgy, effeminate, well-manicured mitts. His enormous belly almost touched her, yet he was two feet away. He was by far the largest man she'd ever seen. He could, no doubt, no longer fit into the cockpit of his World War One fighter. Or probably any fighter, for that matter. Maybe that was why he had his own train?

The leader of the Luftwaffe and high-ranking Nazi listened intently, never taking his eyes off her, while Helmut recounted, in rapid German, her deeds in the air. Goering nodded and clucked, and then he spoke, in perfect English, which startled her. She did not know why.

"How did you enjoy the air exhibition?"

"It was impressive, sir."

"Please, my dear, call me Hermann. There is no rank here. You hear that, Helmut? No rank tonight. We are all one big, happy band. So, Miss Endeavours, are you impressed with our new Luftwaffe?"

"I am, especially the new fighter, the Bf 109.

"Ahh, yes. Our sports car of the air."

"The count here says he can take me up in one."

"Yes, and why not? We want the world to see our latest achievements. The 109 will be the dominant fighter for years to come, to suppress the growing menace of world communism."

"Herr Reichsmarschall, perhaps you would care for some hors d'oeuvres?" the count said.

"I just came from dinner, but yes, now that you mention it." Goering was successfully distracted and veered off to a nearby waiter with a tray of food who was shaking with fear.

"He likes you," the count said.

"I heard I should not be left alone with him."

The count laughed quietly. "Whoever told you that is wrong. The Reichsmarschall has enormous appetites, but by all accounts, he is faithful to his wife. Unlike the rest of the cabal that surrounds the Führer."

"Listen, Helmut, I have to use the facilities."

"Yes, of course. Come this way."

"I can find it on my own. I'm a pretty good navigator." She gave him a smile to take the sting out of the words. "Just point me in the right direction."

"Through those doors and on the left."

"Thank you."

Aubrey left the main reception room, and the din of conversation faded as she walked through a set of double doors. She found the ladies' but skirted by it. She was actually in search of a phone directory. There was a kitchen at the end of the hall, and she saw cooks dashing around and the waiters in their tight white jackets and black pants balancing even more trays of food and drink. There was a set of stairs, and she ascended to the second story.

After checking that she was alone, Aubrey cautiously engaged in bit of snooping. Most of the rooms were either enormous bedrooms or completely devoid of furniture. She finally happened upon the count's office, where she saw a bronze head of Hitler on an enormous oak desk. There were papers strewn about on it, and she glanced at them briefly, remembering her mission. They were covered in figures; industrial output numbers. They made no sense to her, but she was sure if she studied them, they would be of some value to the Brits and her uncle.

She was not stupid enough to pick them up. She was here for one thing only: to make contact with this agent of Hewitt's, retrieve what he had to give her and get out. Still, she slid one document out and saw what she thought were kilometres per hour at various altitudes. Very useful. But no. She slid it back into the pile.

She opened a desk drawer and saw a book. A quick flip through it showed that it was a phone directory, very similar to an American version. She turned to the F's, scanning for Frick, and saw one entry in Wannsee. She memorized the address, 32 Eindhoven Strasse, and the phone number. She closed the book with a slap and then froze. Someone was there.

"What exactly are you doing there?" a voice called into the room, chilling her to the bone.

She turned, half expecting it to be the count, praying it would be. It was worse, much worse. Captain Schmidt stood in the doorway, his chest and chin thrust forward in accusation. He strode over to her.

"I said, what are you doing in here? At the count's personal desk?"

"I was looking for the bathroom. I just wandered in."

The SS captain took one look at the papers on the desk and realized their importance. "You were spying."

"I was not. I'll be honest, I was looking for a phone book. Found one." She tapped the book.

"You were spying. These are classified documents."

"Then why does the count have them on his desk?"

The SS man moved uncomfortably close and grabbed one of her biceps. "You were spying."

"No, not true. I wasn't, honest."

His eyes bored into her as he spoke. "The tulips in Amsterdam were quite brilliant this year."

She was dumbfounded; she couldn't believe it. That was the sign she and Hewitt Purnsley had gone over and over again. It was Starlight's identifying sign. Now here he was, this Hauptsturmführer of the SS, waiting for the countersign.

He gritted his teeth and repeated it. Her brain scrambled for the reply. She gave it.

"I prefer the red poppies of Flanders."

He came back quickly with the third countersign. "The lilies of Poland can be delightful too."

And she gave him the fourth: "Nothing compares to the forget-me-nots of Germany." She stared at him. "You? You're the person Hewitt—"

"Keep your voice down," he hissed. "I followed you up here."

"You have something for me?"

"What were you doing here?"

"Just like I said, looking for a phone book. I have a friend from school who has relatives in Wannsee. She asked me to check on them."

"You're lucky I was the only one who caught you snooping in the count's personal rooms."

"It's all true—you can come with me if you want. I have the address." She was babbling now, she realized, and she willed herself to calm down.

There was the slam of car doors outside on the driveway. The SS captain went to the window. "The Reichsmarschall is leaving. I should be downstairs." He turned his attention back to Aubrey. "You are under surveillance all the time. This little escapade could have gotten you caught, and that would have exposed me."

"How? I didn't know you were Starlight until you identified yourself. And speaking of that, I thought you were going to give me something."

He rifled through his pants pocket. "How will you get it out of Germany?"

"The SIS took care of that."

"Very well. Here." He went to hand her a slip of white paper. There was a noise outside the office, and he quickly pulled his hand back and stuffed the note back in his pocket just as the count entered the office.

"There you are, Aubrey. Captain Schmidt, I didn't know you were up here."

"Sorry, I got lost, Helmut. I found the ladies' and then I needed a phone book." Again, she patted the leather-bound book.

"You are welcome in my home, Aubrey, but this office is private."

"Herr Count von Villiez, it would be remiss of me not to point out that you have seemingly classified material strewn about your desk," Schmidt said.

"What are you accusing me of?"

"Nothing, Count. Just a friendly bit of advice."

The count moved behind his desk, scooped the papers into the drawer and locked it. Aubrey handed over the phone book.

Helmut said, "Why didn't you just ask?"

"I forgot. Spur-of-the-moment thing. The young officer here checked up on me."

Schmidt cut her off. "We should rejoin the Reichsmarschall. He is preparing to leave."

"Agreed." The trio left the office and the count locked the door. He let the SS man get ahead of him and pulled Aubrey back.

"Are you all right?"

"He just scared me is all. He thought I was spying."

"You weren't, were you?"

"Of course not. Like I said, I was just looking for a phone book. I apologize for going into your office, but I'm no spy."

"Good, because in Germany spies are dealt with harshly."

"I'll bet."

12

The count escorted Aubrey back into the party. There were women there now, a half dozen mingling among the forty men. Goering kissed the hand of one of them and then was escorted out of the house.

The rest of the women were scattered throughout the soiree, drinking and laughing. Aubrey didn't need to be hit over the head to realize they had all been purchased and provided by the count.

"It is how business is done, my dear. I would not have been able to sell a thing to this lot without first greasing the wheels."

"I don't mind. As long as they don't think I'm for sale."

"Never. Everyone knows who you are. Still, I understand how it might make you uncomfortable. It is disrespectful to you. I apologize." He looked genuinely abashed.

"It has been a long day; would you have your car take me back to my hotel?"

"But of course."

The count escorted her out to the Mercedes and apologized profusely for not seeing her home personally.

"Nonsense. You have a party to attend to, and a load of important people in there. I'll see you tomorrow at the exhibition?" she asked, throwing the count a bone.

"I do not know yet. I have important work to do. Perhaps we could dine tomorrow night?"

"Sounds fine."

"I'll leave a message at your hotel with the details."

13

Aubrey opened the door to her room and stood for a moment, looking around. The quilt was still hastily thrown over the bed the way she'd left it; the maid had definitely not been in to tidy up. Aubrey stood there, breathing in through her nose, trying to detect if someone had been in the room. Body odour, perhaps aftershave or cologne if a spy or security agent had been careless.

She was in full spy mode now, which, as Hewitt Purnsley had stressed, she should be. Switched on. That introduction to the agent in the count's manor house was still fresh in her mind. It had rocked her to the core, largely because of who Purnsley's agent had turned out to be. That young Nazi officer with the eyes of a killer was betraying his country? Or was he? He had never actually handed her anything. It could all be a trap, with the real spy rotting away in the basement of Gestapo headquarters.

No, she told herself, *don't overthink it. The man has his reasons for doing what he's doing.* Hewitt had only touched on the methods used to make a man betray his country. The leverage, the manipulation. They did it for money or a feeling of power or to get back at their higher-ups for not recognizing their value.

Sometimes a person betrayed his country purely for the sake of ideology. But the man was a uniform-wearing, card-carrying, Heil Hitler–saluting Nazi. One of the SS, an organization totally committed to Hitler's world vision. Could a man such as that grow disillusioned? Enough to risk his life and that of his family?

The last reason Hewitt Purnsley had talked about was sexual compromise. He'd called it a honey trap. Explained how it worked over coffee their last night alone in a quite café on the Right Bank.

Sex, one of humanity's oldest motivators, could be used to compromise someone, with either a member of the opposite sex or, even better, of the same sex. The threat of exposure of homosexuality was a powerful motivator, especially in an organization such as the SS. Aubrey had asked boldly, "Do you want me to tart it up in Germany?" Hewitt had told her no, under no circumstances was she to explore any kind of relationship with any German.

Yet here she was, exploring it, in her heart at least, with the Count von Villiez. She had been able to think of nothing else on the drive back to the hotel. That old sensation, gone for a long time now, had never really established itself except for a brief fling in St. Louis when she had been flying. There was no mistaking it now, though: it was coming on strong. Aubrey was developing real feelings for the dashing aristocrat and captain of industry.

She flicked on the lights to banish her girlish thoughts and moved around the room examining the tells she'd left, little markers that might indicate if someone had been in her room and gone through her things, as meagre as they were.

Hewitt had talked about indicators good operatives used to identify whether a room had been entered. She'd mentioned a scene she'd seen in a movie: a match stuck into the door jamb to indicate whether someone had been there. If the door had been opened, the match would have been lying on the floor.

He'd warned her not to use that trick. It took training to do it right. Besides, much like she wasn't supposed to let someone tailing her know she was on to them, a match in the door jamb would also reveal her tradecraft. No, he'd had something else in mind, and they'd gone over it thoroughly. She'd employed it just before she'd left her room earlier that day.

She'd picked one of the legs of her bed, the one at the foot, closest to the door. Then she'd placed several personal items around the room, aligning them in a specific way with that post. If they had been examined, they would likely be moved when they were set back in place. After all, no one was going to suspect Aubrey of being a master spy. If the Abwehr, Germany's intelligence service, or the Gestapo had sent someone into her room, it might be an amateur such as herself.

She'd also left out a copy of *Harper's Weekly Gazette,* with a picture of a beautiful starlet swinging on a trapeze on the cover. One of the starlet's feet was pointed at the bedpost. As far Aubrey she could tell, it had not been moved. There were other indicators, too: her makeup bag and her two pieces of luggage were all lined up with the bedpost, just the way she'd left them. Her father's pistol was still under the mattress. She retrieved it. It was loaded, but lacked one up the spout, as her father would say. She put it back in her bag, within arm's reach if she needed it. Thoughts of Captain Schmidt, "Starlight" or not, and his goons breaking down the door in the middle of the night were not beyond the realm of possibility. With that, Aubrey got ready for bed and switched off the lights.

14

From the window of the car, Aubrey could see the dark plume of smoke coming from the Luftwaffe air base a mile away. She recognized the mushroom cloud–like shape of an explosion. The sight of one of those at an air base, any air base, usually meant there had been a crash. This much smoke usually resulted in the death of a pilot.

She shuddered as it billowed up into the air. She'd seen that before, all too often. One time in particular it had meant the death of a close friend, a man she could easily have fallen in love with. Her heart sank and her neck tightened in anticipation as they approached the gates of the air base. A fire truck roared by, its bell clanging, firefighters on the back of it hanging on for dear life.

She was in a taxi this morning. She had pleaded with the count for the two young airmen to be called off Aubrey duty. She would manage fine with a taxi. The count had argued but confirmed that he would make it so. A taxi had been arranged through the hotel. She'd looked back once or twice to see if she was being tailed, but could not spot anything unusual. This gave her little comfort; her training with Hewitt Purnsley had been rushed, and they hadn't gotten to this aspect of counter-surveillance.

The entrance to the airfield was deserted; everyone had rushed to the crash. Nevertheless, she took her credentials out of her purse and put them around her neck. She even found a registration book and signed in. The guards were hurrying back when she passed through the gates. She waved her credentials at them but they seemed uninterested.

The smoke cloud had lost its unique mushroom shape and was being carried towards Berlin. A continuous upstream of black smoke was feeding it, and now she could see flames at ground level. Aviation fuel burned ferociously, usually reducing any human remains to charred embers. The smell hit her now: a mixture of spent fuel, burnt metal and paint, and human flesh. She was transported back in time to that airfield outside of St. Louis and the sight of a burgeoning love being burned to a crisp while she was restrained by her fellow pilots. She shook her head. *That was a long time ago, Aubrey. A different world, a different life. Get in the game.*

The crash this morning had happened at the end of the tarmac, and two fire trucks were dousing the inferno. Aubrey could see the wreckage of at least two planes. The fire trucks, one manned by Luftwaffe personnel and the civilian one that had passed her on the street, were aggressively attacking the fire. It was getting dangerously close to a row of parked aircraft. Luftwaffe crew scrambled over those aircraft, removing blocks and hooking up a tow to the one nearest to the flames that crept along the grass. The scene was half-pandemonium, with officers shouting orders and the firefighters directing their hoses here and there. The civilians in attendance were frozen in place, struggling to comprehend what they were witnessing. Civilians like Richard Fuchs, who was just standing there amongst his fellow journalists, holding his hat in his hand.

She sprinted over to him. "What happened?" she asked.

He barely glanced at her and answered in German. "A crash. What do you think happened?" Then he realized who he was addressing. "Two planes collided in mid-air; I saw the whole thing. It was like it was happening in slow motion. One was able to land. The other fell on the aircraft parked there. The pilot is dead, I would imagine. They haven't been able to get to him."

"He's gone," she said.

"You've seen this sort of thing before?"

"Too many times."

"I don't know how you can look at it. It's bloody awful."

"You're a journalist. Aren't you supposed to be able to handle things like this?"

He scoffed. "I guess. So, how was last night?" he said, changing the subject. "Where did His Grace take you?"

"To his home."

"And you think *I* move fast."

"There was a reception. I met Hermann Goering."

"Ahh, I see." He looked at his shoes then back up to her. "On a whim, I went to your hotel. I was nearby. I waited an hour and then another to see if you would come back. Got more than a little drunk at the hotel bar. I cursed your name."

"Are you still cursing it?"

"No. I was a little dry this morning, hung over." He nodded at the scene, the rising smoke. "Not any more. I'm sorry, but I have to go file this."

"I understand." She needed to do the same thing, she realized. She wondered how she would write it. She wanted at least some of the truth of her mission here to make it into the American magazines. If it were discarded by the ghost writers and editors in charge of publishing her articles on her behalf, so be it. At least she would have tried.

There was no point in sticking around. She did not see the count, and the exhibition would surely be closed today. She hitched a ride back into the nearest town, and from there, with her rudimentary German, she managed to catch a taxi that was willing to drive her to Wannsee. She had plenty of money and had to show it up front before he agreed.

She got halfway there when she remembered to check for a tail. It was difficult to do this discreetly in the taxi, but again she was fairly certain no one was behind her. She would put her brief training to the test when she got to Wannsee and started walking around. She had the picture of the girl with her; she'd tucked it into her handbag before leaving the hotel, knowing that today, or at least soon, she would try and find her.

The Frick house was not far from the count's stately manor. It was less impressive in size, but it still spoke of wealth and privilege. A gardener working the hedges near the entrance paid Aubrey no mind when she came up the path.

A stern-looking woman, as thin as a rail with horn-rimmed glasses, opened the door and looked down her nose at Aubrey.

"I'm looking for Lydia Frick. Does she live here?"

"Who are you?"

"A friend of Lydia's, from America. It's important that I see her. Is she here?"

"No, not anymore."

"They moved away?"

"Leave our property at once or I will call the police." The woman glanced past Aubrey to see if anyone was watching. Then she slammed the door. The abruptness of it pushed Aubrey off the steps, and she stood there dumbfounded. There was no use knocking again; she would get a sterner reply and probably that police intervention. She had no choice but to leave.

As she neared the gate, the gardener moved even closer to it. He spoke to her without raising his head from his work.

"You're looking for Lydia?"

"I am."

"I was their gardener for twenty years. They've gone."

"I got that impression. They moved out of Berlin?"

"Not moved. *Were* moved. They are still in Berlin, last I heard."

"Where are they?"

"Jewish Quarter. They wrote to me. They are in a house on Eindhoven Strasse; I don't know the number. I threw the letter away."

"Do you want me to give them a message?"

Aubrey heard the sound of the front door opening again, and the gardener turned his back on her and moved farther down the hedges.

The row houses on Eindhoven Strasse could have been anywhere in the US; St. Louis, Chicago, Brooklyn. What was striking about this area of town was the absence of children. Absence of any signs of life, really. The street was deserted; shutters closed quickly as she passed from house to house.

The other thing striking about this street compared to others in Wannsee was the garbage. There were piles of it on the street corners and in front of the houses, where the other streets were spotlessly clean. She could see where rats had chewed into the paper bags to get at the contents. It looked like the rubbish collection had been suspended in this area.

There was a synagogue on the corner. Outside it, two loutish-looking goons in brown shirts with swastika armbands were hanging around, writing down the license plate numbers of what few worshipers there were, it being Friday.

She went up to the front door of one of the houses and knocked. A man answered, and she asked for the Fricks. The man shook his head. "Number 29," he said. He seemed relieved she wasn't enquiring about him, happy to direct the attention of this foreigner elsewhere.

She climbed the steps of 29 and knocked. She saw a tarnished mezuzah on the door post. There was a shuffling sound on the other side of the door and a woman called out faintly, asking who was bothering her. The door opened a crack, and an elderly woman, hunched over with a mole on her face, peered out.

"Ja?"

Aubrey asked after Lydia.

"She's not here. At work."

"Where does she work?"

"The bakery. Where else. Who are you?" Aubrey noticed milky-white cataracts on both of the woman's eyes.

"A friend of a friend."

"You're not German."

"No, American."

That made no impression on the woman.

"What time will she be home?"

"I don't know."

"Where is the bakery?"

The woman huffed and slammed the door as hard as her frail body could manage. Aubrey stood there, her ears ringing. Two door slams in less than an hour. She descended to the street and looked around. Farther down, she saw a middle-aged Hassidic Jew in a straight-rimmed black hat. The long tendrils of his payot hung down on either side of his face, and the rope-like *tzitzit* dangled from under his black coat.

She approached him. He had his nose buried in a book of prayer as he walked, but became aware of her and backed up.

"Excuse me," she said, "I'm looking for a bakery in this area of the city. Is there one nearby?"

The man stepped out into the street to avoid her, holding up the book of prayer to fend her off.

"I don't mean to frighten you. I just want to know where the bakery is. I'm looking for someone."

The man hurried off, skirting far into the street to get around her.

"There is one farther up the street," someone called. She turned to look.

The man was young, younger than Aubrey, but he was confident, cocky. He was leaning up against the lamppost across the street. He hadn't been there a second ago.

"This way, you said?" she asked, pointing in the direction she'd been walking.

"Yes." He spoke English. "What's a foreigner doing in this place?"

She crossed the street to him. "I'm a journalist."

"Come to witness the end?"

"No, I—what?"

"It's dangerous here for you," he said.

Just then there was the sound of a drum from farther up the street, and a squad of men in those same brown shirts and dark pants rounded the corner four abreast. They were marching, swastika flags held in front of them. One was pounding on a bass drum.

"Come on, you must get off the street," the young man said urgently. "They are SA men—the Sturmabteilung."

"But—" Aubrey said.

The man grabbed her hand and hauled her into a vacant yard, bordered on three sides with a wooden fence. There was a gate, almost invisible until the young man wrenched it open.

"Quick—in here."

Aubrey stepped through. The squad of brownshirts passed, their voices raised angrily in song.

"Why are you looking for Jewish pastry in this part of Berlin, American journalist?" the young man said.

"Do you know this girl?" She showed him the photograph. The man showed no recognition. "The bakery is just down the street, you said. I was told she works there."

"Leave this area of Berlin, miss. It is too dangerous."

"Thank you, but not until I speak to her. I made a promise of sorts."

The man peered out the gate and was satisfied the brownshirts had gone away. Then he was through the makeshift gate and gone, back the way the SA squad had come from. He made no indication that Aubrey was to follow him. Besides, he was too fast for her. He probably had to be, given all that was going on here.

"Nice talking to you, Aubrey," she said to herself. "Yeah, real helpful."

She walked along the street in the direction the young man had indicated, and soon found herself in a row of shops. Aubrey strolled along, looking in the windows at the goods for sale. She first smelled then saw the bakery. It was open and had a line out the door; most of the men were dressed like the Hassidic Jew she'd encountered.

She passed by the bakery and made a concerted effort to look in the other shops. Many of them had crudely painted six-point stars on the windows. Some windows were boarded up, and there were glittering shards of glass here and there on the pavement. When she looked in the Jewish shops, she could see store owners behind their counters, their faces masks of despair. One or two saw her, smiled and nodded. She nodded back, although right now her window shopping was not just a show of support for the oppressed Jewish community.

As Purnsley had taught her in their brief time together, she was using the windows to spot a tail. And spot one she did. The young man she'd spoken to a few minutes earlier was behind her. He wasn't as good as the seasoned man from British Intelligence.

She saw a break in the traffic and dashed across the street—not running away, just trying to avoid being hit by a truck or car or one of the constantly passing trams. She headed back in the direction of the bakery. Again she slowed, pausing at a store front. He was still there, behind her, hands in his pockets, pausing when she did, resuming when she started moving again. She saw him give a quick shake of his head to someone unseen. He put his hand out and waved it down at the sidewalk in a dismissive gesture. A tram came by, its bell clanging, letting out a moan as it slowed to let a lorry with canvas sides clear the tracks.

An open-sided truck filled with brown-shirted thugs weaved its way down the street, deliberately sliding out into the opposing traffic, causing everything to come to a stop as it came chugging by. She heard horns honking and trumpets blaring; the men in the truck were singing, all waving that hideous flag.

The intimidation was palpable as they passed. Then, after it had rounded a corner, the citizens quietly resumed what they had been doing. Up ahead, Aubrey saw a tram that was just pulling away from a station. She broke into a jog and caught the rear door. A man held out his hand and helped her up. She could come back to the bakery later, maybe spot Lydia and catch up with her on her way home from work. Right now, though, she had to lose this tail.

The attendant was in the front section of the articulated tram and she fumbled for the ten-Reichsmark coin to put into his can. She glanced back at the road; the young man who had been following her was nowhere to be seen.

A kind gentleman offered her a seat, and she was able to watch the shops, buildings and cathedrals roll by. She spotted more brownshirts on foot or in trucks. Several of them got on board the tram and talked excitedly amongst themselves while the other passengers kept quiet and avoided eye contact.

Aubrey realized she was heading away from her hotel, out of the city, so after five stops she got off with the intention of getting a taxicab back to the Jewish quarter. There were none in sight; they usually had stands out in front of hotels, and she could see some taller buildings in the distance. One of them might be a hotel.

She turned a corner and came face to face with the man who had first saved her from the brownshirt marching squad and then tailed her around the quarter. *How the devil?* He came at her fast. She turned. There was a car pulling up alongside of her, exhaust puffing out of the tailpipe. Its door opened, and a second man got out and came up behind her; she'd spotted him getting on the tram earlier. They were together, the two of them.

She tightened her grip on her purse. She could swing it at the lead one, maybe punch the other. She'd thrown a punch or two in her time. Suddenly she realized how quiet the street was, how secluded.

"What do you want?" she asked the first man.

"Get in the car."

"I'm not going anywhere with you."

"You want to see Lydia? We'll take you to her."

Aubrey looked at both men. At least they didn't look like Nazis. The one behind her was definitely Jewish; he reminded her somehow of a girl she'd gone to school with in Rockingham. Dorothy Bass. He had the same features.

She dropped her shoulders and got into the rear seat of the car. The two men got in up front; the first man drove now. If only she'd had her father's gun with her, she thought unhappily, she would show them a thing or two. It would be worth it just to see the looks on their faces when she pressed the tip of the barrel to the driver's ear.

The car smelled of mould, and a spring in the seat poked her in the thigh. The young man drove fast, swerving in and out of the tram lines and around corners at a blistering clip. The other one looked out the back window continuously. Aubrey did not sense danger from these men but knew if they were caught together by the German authorities, it would go badly for her. For all of them.

Eventually, with a hard turn they drove up to a workshop in an industrial area of East Berlin. The car roared into a disused warehouse, the metal door was closed behind them and the car was engulfed in darkness.

Aubrey and the two men got out of the car. Someone switched on the overhead lights, revealing a grimy workshop of lathes and drill presses. The floor was covered in sawdust, and the air was thick with the smell of industrial lubricants. A half dozen people appeared at the edges of the darkness, afraid to reveal themselves.

"Nice place," Aubrey said to the man who'd tailed her. "Why have I been kidnapped?"

"You haven't been kidnaped. You've merely accompanied us. Why are you making enquiries about a girl you clearly don't know?"

"How do you know I don't know her?"

"Because I don't know *you*," a female voice called from the darkness. One of the shapes on the periphery emerged. It was Lydia from the photograph. Aubrey didn't need to look at it to confirm it.

"I've never met you in my life," Lydia said.

"Nor I you. I was given this." Aubrey held up the picture. The girl came closer and took it. Like the driver of the car, she was both young and old at the same time. It fascinated Aubrey, and saddened her. Before all this, she'd thought of herself as worldly, having seen more of life and death than all the pupils of Rockingham Girls' Collegiate put together.

Lydia studied the photo, then turned it over and read the back.

"How did you get this?"

"A man I met in Belgium gave it to me. He said to tell you, Lydia, that he died a free man."

Lydia looked at her in surprise. "Leave us," she said to the others.

"But Lydia..." The driver spoke in German to her, and they had a lightning-fast exchange; Aubrey could not follow it. She caught only two words: "Gestapo" and "traitor."

Finally, the two men who'd brought Aubrey to the warehouse went reluctantly off into the darkness with the others. Aubrey and Lydia stood there in the cone of light from the weak bulb hanging overhead.

The young German girl tucked the photo into her own pocket. Aubrey did not mind; it had served its purpose.

"Tell me about him," Lydia said.

"Not much I can say. He died."

There was a sigh from the girl. She looked at the floor and then back at Aubrey.

"But he made it out. At least that's something."

"I was with him when he died. He gave me that picture. I kind of made a promise to him."

"To find me, to return it?"

"No. He mentioned a man named Lazarus. Said that he should be gotten out as well."

Lydia nodded, her face carefully blank.

"What was the real name of the man who died? He wouldn't tell me."

"Eckhart. We were lovers. We were to be married. My father did not approve."

"Why did Eckhart have to flee the country?"

"He is—was—part of a group who are trying to change things. I am part of that same group. And the others." She gestured at the shadowy figures. "They alerted me that someone was trying to find me. We have to be careful; the Gestapo are not averse to using women to track us down. We resist the ruling party. They want to crush us for it."

"Resist how?"

"There are some of my people who want to try and seek out an accommodation with the state." Lydia shook her head. "They are fools. As the noose tightens around our necks, it tightens around theirs, too. They're just too stupid to realize it."

"But not you?"

"We resist. We fight back."

"How can you? The Nazis are so powerful."

"What choice do we have?"

"Get out, like Eckhart did."

"Tell me, are you a spy? I know Eckhart was working with the British."

"I'm an American."

"But are you a spy?"

"I suppose so." She paused, watching for Lydia's reaction. "Now there's a little secret in exchange for yours."

That brought a smile to the girl's face for the first time. "You are playing a dangerous game. You have no idea what the state is capable of if they catch you."

"They'll send me to Dachau?"

Lydia stared at her. "How do you know of that?"

"I've heard of it. It sounds horrific."

"It is. It's one of a series of camps the SS set up after Hitler was elected. The state refers to them euphemistically as protective custody. We may all wind up there, if they don't gun us down first. Tell me, though, what are you doing here? Why did you need to find me? To return a photograph?"

"I'm here because of Lazarus."

"What of him?"

"Do you know him?"

"He is my father. They have him in a camp not far from here."

"What did your father do? Was he a politician opposed to the Nazis?"

"My father is Dr. Tomei Lazarus Frick. Everyone calls him by his middle name. He is a scientist. A brilliant man—theoretical physics."

"Ah, yes. Your fiancé mentioned that."

"He was working at the Berlin university when Hitler came to power. Lost his position almost overnight. Good friends and colleagues, all refused to speak up for him. He started making speeches, working with the Jewish organizations. One by one, these organizations have been obliterated, and the Nazis came for my father a year ago. Dragged him from our home. I haven't seen him since."

"All attempts to find out what has happened to him are met with blank stares or, worse, threats. We only know the camp he's in. We received a letter, not in his handwriting, telling us everything was fine, that he was getting a better understanding of what it means to be a good German. That's when I started to resist, joined the movement." She paused. "You've done your duty to Eckhart, Miss..."

"Endeavours. Aubrey Endeavours."

"You shouldn't have told me that."

Aubrey shrugged.

"You can go now," Lydia said. "One of my friends will drive you to a tram that will take you back to your hotel. Just tell him where you are staying."

"No, wait—please. I made a promise to Eckhart when he was dying. He said that Lazarus must be set free. Maybe I can help."

"I don't see how you can help. None of us can do anything for him. He's as good as dead."

"That's a hell of a way to speak about your own father."

"It's our reality. This is my world now." She waved her hands around at the darkness. "Here, I am safe, like a rat. At least for the time being. Go back to America, Miss Endeavours. Tell them what you saw in Berlin. Not that anyone will give a damn."

15

Richard Fuchs was propping up the short zinc bar in the hotel's lobby. He was sipping steaming tea out of a silver *podstakannik* cup holder.

"That looks perfect. I wouldn't mind one," Aubrey said. "How long have you been here?"

"Two cups of tea."

"Don't you want anything stronger?"

"No, not me, I'm afraid. I don't take it well. It's genetic." He looked around the lobby. "This is a charming hotel. I come here often. Shall we get a bite to eat? I know an equally charming restaurant nearby."

Aubrey didn't respond. She was distracted by the sleek shape of Count von Villiez's Mercedes Benz pulling up in front of the hotel. Fuchs turned to see what had caught her eye just as Helmut entered the hotel. The count studied the lobby; his long grey trench coat was thrown over his shoulder like a cape. His chin thrust out at a commanding attitude. He spied Aubrey at the bar and waved a leather-gloved hand at her.

"I've been trumped again," Fuchs muttered.

"Count von Villiez, so nice to see you again," Aubrey said. "This is my friend Richard Fuchs."

"How do you do?" the count said, as though just realizing someone else was at the bar. Aubrey felt a twinge of irritation. She had no time for men who put on airs. Relax, Aubrey, she told herself. It's just a game men play.

"Your Excellency, we have never been formally introduced, but..."

"But you know me?"

"I work for the *Berliner Morgenpost*."

"Oh." The count chuckled, not quite nervously, but not in amusement either. He turned to Aubrey. "My dear, you're drinking with the enemy. Well, at least he *was* the enemy until his newspaper developed the proper attitude."

"What's he mean, Richard?" Aubrey stared at Fuchs in puzzlement.

"We ran a series of articles about the count's business dealings a few years back, when we still had such freedom." He looked back at the count. "Your Grace, I hope you do not harbour resentment. I know only too well what resentment can bring these days." He got to his feet. "Aubrey, *auf wiedersehen*." He deposited some crumpled Reichsmark notes on the zinc bar and left.

"What was that all about?" Aubrey said.

"His paper has learned who's in charge. Its reporters may chafe, but if they want to keep their jobs, and more importantly their necks..." The count trailed off.

Aubrey fidgeted uncomfortably.

"I'm not entirely on side with it, Aubrey. I want you to know that. I've always enjoyed a good piece of journalistic investigative work; just not when it was directed at me personally."

"I understand."

"Good. So, dinner?"

"I was going to retire early."

"Nonsense. I feel like shrugging off these blues. The tragedy at the airfield has had me in a funk all day. I require your assistance in banishing it. I offer you a grand tour of Berlin, warts and all." He held out his arm.

Aubrey slipped her hand into the crook of his elbow. "A girl can't pass that up, now, can she?"

16

The crack of the whip startled Aubrey. She was feeling the benumbing effect of a succulent dinner of Norwegian crab legs paired with a crisp Riesling from the Rhineland, plus countless shots of schnapps. At first the count had been skeptical about her drinking prowess. Then a begrudging respect had grown. Now she seemed to be taking the lead in the matter. Helmut looked to be going down for the count, so to speak. Thankfully, this was their last stop for the evening. It had better be, she thought. Dawn was fast approaching.

The lazy jazz music of the subterranean Rathskeller he had taken her to at midnight had only added to the sleepy effects of the dinner. She had watched Helmut's chin start to fall to his chest.

But when the woman, clad in a black leather vest and mid-thigh skirt complete with a twelve-foot-long bullwhip, walked onstage, things had picked up. She cracked the whip again, and a man was hurtled onto the stage from the wings. He was dressed in a sailor's uniform and aped being as drunk as Aubrey and the count and the rest of the club-goers actually were. He crashed into the whipmaster, and she shoved him to the ground.

"Oh my," Aubrey said.

Helmut came alive. "What have I missed?"

"Nothing yet," Aubrey said.

When they'd pulled up to the building, Aubrey had been a little perturbed, even a little panicky. The streets were dark, and they had been surrounded by tall buildings whose business had shut down for the day. Then light had spilled from a cellar doorway in front of them and two people had stumbled out.

"What is this?" Aubrey had asked.

"A vestige of the old Weimar Republic," the count had replied. "Come with me, back into time."

Aubrey had read about nightclubs like these. New York, even at the height of Prohibition, with its speakeasies and flappers, had never seemed as wild as what was going on in Germany. So, when they'd entered the sunken denizen, she'd felt suddenly giddy. Helmut hadn't lied: they had gone back in time. It was just as she'd pictured it. Though try as she might, she could never have pictured the erogenous act that was presently occurring on stage. She turned away and blushed.

Another crack of the whip.

"I'm sorry, my dear. You are offended."

"No, it's just not the sort of thing I'm used to seeing."

The woman with the whip had proceeded to undress the drunken sailor and handcuff him to a chair.

"Surely this isn't allowed?" she said uneasily. "What if it this place gets raided?"

"My dear, in Germany there are arrestable people, all manner of them, and those who are un-arrestable. For the time being, at least, I am one of the latter."

Her eyes had grown accustomed to the smoky scene long ago, but she had avoided looking around at the other patrons. She gave a quick glance at them now; there were no brownshirts in attendance. She imagined that rowdy group confined its hijinks to barracks and beer halls. There were no elite SS either; maybe they had their real-life torture scenes playing out in their dungeons. There were two men in fedoras sitting at the back of the room, watching the whole scene without showing any emotion.

"Are those men back there Gestapo?" she said. "The ones with the hats."

The count saw who she was referring to and laughed.

"No, Aubrey, they are the oldest queer couple in Berlin. This is the only refuge left to them, I suppose. Live and let live, at least in the dark alleyways and basements of the past."

The act concluded with a brief showing of all of the man's attributes; Aubrey's face grew red with embarrassment. Then a woman with a python wrapped around her neck came on stage to raucous applause. She sang with a deep falsetto, and after a while Aubrey clued into the real gender of the singer. Next, a black man at the piano sang in flawless French, a mournful tune about the good old days and a long-lost love. Then the black-clad woman came back with her whip; this time she stepped out into the audience, tantalizing and flirting and teasing both men and women.

She grabbed the count by the tie, and Aubrey thought he was going to be pulled on stage. But then the dominatrix turned her attentions to her, running her hand delicately across Aubrey's face and down her bosom. Aubrey sat there rock still, as scared as the rabbits that she knew must be fed to the python. Thankfully, the woman moved on to another table.

"She's something, isn't she? You should have seen her in her heyday," the count said when they were back in the Benz.

Safely ensconced in the confines of the big Mercedes, with the thick velvet curtain pulled across the partition, the count finally pulled Aubrey into his arms. She did not resist.

17

Aubrey woke up in a sea of silk pillows and sheets and a thick duvet. She lay in the enormous bed in the count's master bedroom, staring at the plaster scrollwork on the ceiling. A warm glow flooded through her when she thought of the previous night; the tender moments in the bed, the weight of him pressing down on her. The first time had been rushed, in the back seat of the Mercedes as they roared to the count's home at a hundred miles an hour. The second time, she'd led him by the tie up the stairs, and then they were ensconced in this tumble of sheets, rising to ecstasy again and again.

She ran her hand over to his side of the large mattress, found the sheets cold. She smiled at the comfort of the place and the memories of everything they'd done. Propped up on both elbows, she surveyed the room; it had been in darkness when they'd first entered earlier that morning.

The room was white everywhere: the furniture, the walls and ceilings. The walls were white paper with thin gold lines that flashed in the morning light streaming in through the open windows. There was a balcony with an espresso table and a set of chairs, all white. There was gold jewellery, a tie pin and cuff links scattered on a white cloth on top of the large dresser. Her clothes were folded neatly on a chair instead of heaped on the floor where she'd left them. How thoughtful. A thick robe lay on another chair, and a doorway led to an en-suite bathroom.

The air felt cold against her skin when she sprang from the bed and dashed to the bathroom, grabbing the robe as she went. Hot needles of water tickled her flesh in the shower. She held herself, all soapy and warm again, and ran her hand down her belly to between her legs. She fantasized about the count coming into the shower behind her and embracing her, pressing his hardness against her. She wondered if he was still in the house. She dried herself off with a plush towel and wrapped herself in the robe.

There was a knock at the door. The count? No, he wouldn't knock, although he might knock and enter simultaneously. This was his room, and Aubrey had nothing left to hide from him. Another knock: the light knuckle-rap of a female.

Aubrey bade the person to come in. She recognized the maid from the soiree the count had thrown. The young girl was carrying a tray of delicious-looking buttered buns and bacon and a pot of tea. She spoke to Aubrey in German. Aubrey's brain was still buzzing; she didn't bother to try and interpret it. The woman put the tray outside on the balcony after not receiving a reply.

Aubrey's watch showed nearly noon. This wasn't breakfast; it was brunch. Here it was, the last day of the air exhibition, and she was playing hookey. As if on cue, a very fast airplane roared overhead, a white contrail extending behind it. Perhaps a Bf 109? She remembered Helmut's promise of a ride in one. Then she remembered her mission. If Hewitt Purnsley was sitting beside her, he would say "You damn fool, you silly girl. Lounging around in a German's bed."

But what would he say if he knew she was on the cusp of obtaining real, firsthand knowledge of the 109's capabilities? What better way of finding out than to actually take one up in the air, feel the throb of the stick between her legs, the thunder of the engine, as she rolled that sucker over into a dive to find out what it could handle? Huh, Hewitt Purnsley? How about that? She was confident that when the count took her up, he would let her take the controls. Hang in there, she told herself. This is the way forward. Forget hustling over to the airfield to catch the last of the speeches and sales pitches. Stick with the count: he'll get you up in the damn thing. That might make up for the failed meeting with Agent Starlight. A shiver of fear ran down her back when she thought of the blond-haired spy and his aborted attempt at passing her information. She wondered what the man had had for her. It's not for you, Aubrey, she reminded herself. It's for Hewitt and John Walton.

Aubrey dressed and descended to the lobby. A butler appeared with a note on a silver platter.

My dearest Aubrey,

My work called me away early this morning and I did not want to wake you. Wilbur will ensure you get back to your hotel. I would like to have dinner with you again this evening, if possible. I can meet you at your hotel at 8. If this is not convenient, please inform Wilbur. But I do so desperately hope that it is.

Until later, my love,
Helmut

When she returned to the Hotel Adlon, she had an inclination to get changed and head over to the air exhibition for the last few hours. If Captain Schmidt was there, he might be able to pass on whatever information he had this time.

The more distance and time she put between herself and the count's bedroom and the things that had happened in there, the more doubts she had. The smart thing to do, Aubrey, she told herself, would be to get your things and get on a train out of here. Perhaps even leave the gun behind for some lucky traveller to find, or a maid, lest she be caught with it at the border.

She felt warm again when she thought of Helmut. It wasn't time to leave Berlin, and in the midst of all this danger and intrigue she felt the cloak of his protection over her. She had funny fantasies of the two of them running away together, perhaps back to America. He would be the most dashing foreigner in all of Sacred, Michigan. They could turn her father's farm into a horse breeding operation, or perhaps an airstrip for a flying school. These wild schoolgirl fantasies made her giggle.

Upon entering her room, Aubrey studied its contents. The feeling that someone had been in here was more prominent now. She checked her markers; her overnight bag was out of alignment with the bedpost. And perhaps one of the American magazines as well. Someone may have been interested in what her reading interests were, whether they were 'aligned' with those of the Reich. The Führer would be out of luck, though. *Harper's Bazaar* rarely ran articles on building a racially pure utopia.

The maid had been in the room; the bed was made. Perhaps she'd jostled these things. Perhaps. A quick lift of the mattress showed the gun was still there, the tip of the barrel pointed towards the bedpost. It hadn't been disturbed.

Aubrey changed and headed down to the lobby. There was one message waiting for her at the front desk. It was from Richard Fuchs, just his name and a phone number. There were several phone booths near the elevators. Aubrey stepped into the farthest one and dialled the number on the paper. A female receptionist answered in lightning-fast German. Aubrey managed to ask to be put through to Richard.

"It's a good thing you caught me," he said. "I was just on my way out of the office. Did you have fun last night?"

"I did. The count took me to this underground--"

"Not over the phone," Fuchs said, interrupting her. "You never know who might be listening, my dear."

"I see. Want to meet for coffee?"

"Or maybe something else." Aubrey detected a slur in his words. "There is a café not far from your hotel. Take the number five tram for four stops. It's a big yellow building, French design. You cannot miss it."

"I'll leave now."

"See you soon."

Aubrey saw Fuchs from a long way off. She wasn't sure, but she thought he was stopping, scanning back the way he'd come. Paranoia? It almost looked like the fieldcraft she and Hewitt Purnsley had practised, but it was subtler than that. Maybe a journalist in Berlin, one who had apparently rankled the ruling class, had a right to be paranoid.

Richard saw her and smiled from across the street. He let a truckload of shouting, hooting SA men and a tram pass before dashing across.

"Been here long?" he asked her breathlessly.

"Two cups and one danish.'"

"Good, aren't they?"

"Better than back home."

"Where is home, my dear?"

There was no challenge in the way he said "my dear." He knew that Aubrey and the count had gone on a date; maybe he suspected much, much more. If he only knew the half of what they'd gotten up to. She could still hear the sharp crack of the whip and smell the leather on the woman from the Rathskeller.

"I'm from Michigan. Little town called Sacred."

"I want to visit America one day. You'll have to write down the best places to go."

"New York, Chicago, New Orleans, San Francisco."

"And of course, this town Sacred. I will be like a pilgrim on the way to Mecca."

"If you want to be bored out of your skull, by all means. How was the rest of the exhibition?"

"Oh, yes, that's right—I did not see you there. I attended this morning. I have all I need for my article. German aviation at its finest, except for the sad little business of the crash. I'll leave that part out."

"That was dreadful. Very unfortunate for such a prestigious event."

"It was. That SS captain, the one who almost stopped you from getting in," he began.

"Yes, I remember him," Aubrey said, and looked away quickly.

"He was furious with the cancelling of the exhibition. It was disgraceful; the loss of two men's lives had ruined the event for the Führer." A woman next to them turned her head at the scornful way Fuchs had used the leader's title.

"You should keep your voice down."

"We mustn't embarrass the almighty Führer in anyway," Richard said, his voice rising. Yes, he was definitely slurring his words, she realized.

"Seriously, how much have you had to drink?"

"Not enough, my dear. Not nearly enough."

"You said you couldn't handle it; I see you weren't joking. Let's get you a coffee. We need to sober you up before you wind up in prison." Aubrey flagged a waiter down.

"Ah, yes—as a guest of our beloved Führer, in one of his nice little holiday camps."

Other customers' heads were turning now.

"If you don't be quiet, I'm leaving. I don't think they would stop at throwing me in jail just because I'm sitting with you."

"No, of course they wouldn't. I'll bet that one there, stuffing her face with crumpet, is going to go rat me out right now. Aren't you?" he said to the lady nearest them.

"That's enough," Aubrey snapped. "My apologies," she said to the woman. "He's been under some stress."

"Okay, okay," he whispered mockingly. "Concentration camps are very nasty places, I hear."

"Me too. I know someone who was sent to one," she said.

He stared at her in astonishment. "You've only been here three days. Who is it? Tell me!"

"Aren't you afraid of guilt by association? I certainly am, with you sitting here drunk and shooting your mouth off."

"Is this person a friend?"

"He's not a friend, not even someone I know. I made a promise once. Seems I won't be able to fulfill it, though. Heck... At least I tried."

"You have my attention now, Fraulein," Fuchs said, leaning towards her, suddenly sober as a judge. "Please tell me what you're talking about."

"Do people get paroled from these camps?" Aubrey asked him. "My understanding is if you go in, you don't come out."

"They do release people. It just takes the right amount of *baksheesh*."

"What's that?"

He rubbed his fingers together and leaned closer, lowering his voice. "As high and mighty as the Reich may wish to appear, they are not beyond corruption. In fact, quite the opposite. The entire thing is corrupt. Government appointees, Aryanization of businesses. They're even talking of kicking undesirables out of their homes and giving them to those of good German stock. Shameful, I know."

"So, you're saying someone can be sprung for a bribe?"

"I am saying that. It would cost a lot, though, depending on the person incarcerated. Plus, you would have to know exactly whom to bribe or you might end up in there with them."

"How much?"

"Who is it?"

"A scientist. A brilliant physicist. Name is..." She hesitated. "...Lazarus. I met his daughter."

"A Jew?"

Aubrey nodded.

"Ahhh, I see. Our short-sighted Führer doesn't want the help of a Jewish scientist, even one that might help him win the coming war."

"It frightens me to hear you say that."

"What, 'the coming war'? Have you ever seen as many people in uniform as there are here in Berlin, or in all of Germany? I haven't. Not since 1918. All those uniforms can only mean one thing. Hitler laid it all out in his book, apparently. I tried to read it once, but it was damned hard to get through; the man is a raving lunatic."

Aubrey got to her feet. "Come on, let's get out of here."

"Fantastic! I know a great little bar."

"I can't stay out long; I have a commitment later tonight."

"With the dashing count?"

"Yes," she said. She dished out the Reichsmarks for the coffees. Fuchs didn't bother to reach for his wallet. It was the custom in Berlin; there was no stigma attached to a woman paying the bill. Or doing almost anything else, for that matter. She'd stopped into a pharmacy the day before and had been amazed to see a woman in a white pharmacist's coat doling out medication. And the hotel night manager was a woman. As chauvinistic as this society appeared, with all the uniforms and the lantern-jawed men strutting around, Germany seemed to be far more advanced than the States when it came to gender roles.

When they stepped outside, it became apparent that Fuchs was intoxicated; he stumbled against Aubrey, and she grabbed him to keep him from tumbling to the pavement.

"You're loaded. Where were you?"

"In a bar, across from where I work. A long lunch. And it hasn't ended."

"I think it has. I should get you home. Where do you live?"

"Can't go there. Not advisable at the moment. I went back to grab my things from the office; that's when you called. As I was leaving, one of our crime beat reporters informed me that they have a warrant out for my arrest."

"Why? What on earth have you done?"

"Written. Things I've written in the past—yesterday, last year. The things that have yet to be written. I'm a disgrace, not worthy of the heavy mantle that has been handed to me." Fuchs chuckled wetly.

"You think quite highly of yourself."

"I don't mean that—you don't understand. I know a quiet place we can get a drink. Come on."

"I'm not going for any drinks; I have a date tonight that I don't intend to be late for. I'm taking you somewhere. Another coffee shop. Just stop shooting your mouth off about the government."

They were walking into a seedier area of Berlin; that was apparent. There were seductively-dressed women standing in dark alcoves talking to men, their hands caressing the men's shirt fronts. Some played the part of seductress well. Others stood back from their conquests, frightened, their clothes simple dresses that might be worn to the market. They looked like scared children. Aubrey recognized them: street walkers. The newcomers to the game and the old hands.

There were also a few shops; Aubrey recognized the outlines of Yiddish writing, signage that had been scraped off to try and save a pane of glass. There were Jewish men in the centre of the street talking. The merchants and the prostitutes, merchants of a different kind, coexisted.

Richard said, "These women, ladies of the night, have recently set up shop here. The security forces are quartering in all undesirables on top of each other. It will make it easier to contain them, and finally crush them."

"We should turn back."

"No. I have friends here. They can help me. I need a place to hide."

There was the sound of glass breaking and shouts back and forth. The men who were talking to the prostitutes looked around wildly and ran off in different directions. The women stood their ground, perhaps realizing there was nowhere else to go. Not for them, at least.

"It's started," Fuchs said. "The revolution. Or counter-revolution!" he shouted drunkenly.

A surge of people came around the corner. All men, heavily built and wearing not the brown shirts and swastika armbands of the SA but workmen's clothes. They sported the same shaved heads as the SA, though, and wore military boots. They carried stout clubs and pickaxe handles. Their disguises were as pathetic as their attitude.

"The SA," Fuchs said. "I'd recognize them anywhere. Stirring up trouble again."

The group of Jewish men were quickly surrounded. There was no hesitation on the part of the SA agents provocateurs. A hideous scene unfolded as the clubs slammed down, again and again, onto the heads of the surrounded men. Aubrey felt weak at the knees.

Richard grabbed her and held her up. "This is serious," he said. "We must get out of here."

"Shouldn't we witness this? You could write about it. So could I."

For the first time since her foray into the German Reich under her phony cover, Aubrey realized her responsibility, journalistic credentials or no. She could see the power of the words she could write about what was going on here. If only she had a camera.

"If we don't move, we're going to get caught up in it," Fuchs said. He started to drag her away, but more men rounded a corner from the opposite direction, cutting off their escape. Aubrey saw a stream of bright red blood flowing into the gutter as the victims tried to crawl away. Clubs rained down on their backs.

"Aubrey, move—now." He tugged her toward a narrow passageway between two buildings. There was the sound of breaking glass and the dull thuds of bricks being hurled after them.

"What is this happening? Why are those men attacking the others?"

"Because they are Jews—it's the only explanation. There are no more communists left to beat up."

He dragged her down the alleyway and out onto a wider street, where there was even more commotion.

"Oh no," she said when they emerged. There was a line of men, more SA in disguise, advancing up the street. Richard looked back the way they had come. He could see the burly, silhouetted shoulders of the mob coming after them. Further up the street was a line of mounted police, fat truncheons in their hands.

"Why don't those police do anything?" Aubrey cried.

"They will. They'll arrest you after you get beaten up."

There was another group of ordinary citizens being pushed down the street by the advancing line of attackers. Some of them brave, maybe stupid, stopped and tried to throw fists at the men with clubs. They were set upon and quickly disappeared into the throng.

A man was on the ground bleeding badly. Aubrey broke away from Richard to try and help the poor man up.

"Aubrey, no—leave him."

The surge of men trying to escape the mob swept past her, carrying Richard with them. The crowd was being pressed in on all sides. Bottles and rocks soared in every direction overhead. She turned to the man she was trying to help, saw the curly locks of a Hassidic Jew hanging over his ears.

"You must go," the man said in a hoarse gurgle. But it was too late: the goons were on them. They separated Aubrey from the man and dragged her away. She saw the Jewish man take a solid blow to the face; his teeth were dashed out onto the street.

Then she was swallowed up by the SA, who called her all manner of nasty things. She couldn't take it all in. She was swirled around and punched solidly in the stomach. It knocked the wind out of her and she collapsed to her knees. A kick to her side and she fell onto the street. The mob continued on, trampling over her. There was the shrieking of police whistles; she smelled the scent of something bitter, and it burned her eyes. Then there was a horse above her; the rider was a policeman wearing a gas mask. He pointed his truncheon at her, spouted something horrific in German, and more police surrounded her. They hauled her to her feet and pinned her hands behind her. She was stuffed in the back of a van, and the door slammed shut.

18

The damp cell held four other women besides Aubrey. One was sobbing incessantly. Another woman, dressed in the garish costume of a prostitute, her face red from drink, shouted at her to stop. The crying woman ceased and rubbed tears away from her eyes. Then her head fell back into her hands and the sobbing resumed.

Aubrey sat next to her on the metal bench, the only one in the squat cell, and put her arm around her. The crying woman jumped and shrank away from her touch. Aubrey got up and went to the bars. She winced when she stood up; there was a sharp pain under her rib cage. She probed it with her fingers and felt the tender spot where the punch had landed, but she didn't think her ribs were busted. She must have a hell of a bruise there. The woman with the red face spoke to her.

"You're American."

Aubrey nodded.

"I heard them say they had a foreigner in the round-up."

"I tried to help someone. My friend and I were separated."

The woman came over. "My name is Helene."

Aubrey introduced herself, just her first name.

"What are you doing in Berlin?"

"I'm doing a story on the state exhibition for aeronautics."

"And you got caught up in the riots, how?"

"I was out seeing the sights. Wrong place, wrong time."

"I know the feeling." The woman burped and Aubrey smelled a disgusting mixture of cabbage and gin. She almost vomited.

The woman had a large belly and was wearing a soiled, frilly nightdress. "I was having a gay old time. I woke up here. They'll let me go soon. They always do."

Aubrey sighed and pushed her face between the bars.

"Don't worry," Helene said. "They won't hold an American long. You'll write bad things about them. They don't want that." She laughed. "Carl," she called, "come let my new friend out. But don't expect a blow job." There was the sound of shuffling footsteps somewhere out of sight.

There had been more women in the cramped cell when Aubrey had first arrived, but steadily, one by one they had been taken out and did not return.

"Where are we?"

"SiPo."

"I don't understand."

"*Sicherheitspolizei*, the security police. SiPo."

"They brought... someone like you... here with the others."

"You mean a whore? It's because I am a bad influence. They want to give me another lecture. Send me underground. What they don't know is that their senior officers are my best customers." She grabbed one of her sagging breasts and hefted it up.

"Carl!" Helene shouted again.

Carl, still unseen, shouted back, "Shut up, Helene. Or you'll get a beating."

There was the clang of a metal doorway and the sound of a stool being knocked over. Carl must have jumped to attention. Two men came into view. They wore the black uniform of the SS and were followed by a man in a police uniform. He was shaking in fear.

"Oh, no, my dear," Helene whispered. "The SD."

One of the men spoke to Carl. He did indeed have that little diamond patch on his sleeve with *SD* stitched inside of it. "We are taking possession of the American." He handed a piece of paper over to Carl. "Unlock the cell and take her out."

Carl fumbled with the keys and got the cell open. Aubrey stepped out. She was marched out of the district SiPo building and put in the back of a large black car. An SS man rode beside her for the short journey across Berlin to Prinz-Albrecht-Strasse. She remembered Hewitt Purnsley mentioning that street name, and the building that resided there.

The car descended into an underground parking garage. There were more SS men there, several carrying submachine guns. Others held just clubs. The door was flung open and Aubrey got out.

"This way," the lead man said in stilted English.

She was led into a bright room. There were men in there, in suits, discussing something and having a smoke. They paused when Aubrey entered. There was an exchange between the suits and the black unforms. Aubrey was hustled down a corridor and locked in a room with a solid door; no bars, just a peephole. There was a metal cot affixed to the wall, but no blanket. She sat down on it; the mattress was soiled and thin, and the springs creaked under her weight. Then Aubrey heard the first of many moans, and what sounded like a terrified scream coming from somewhere else in the building.

She knew where she was: 1195 Prinz-Albrecht-Strasse. She was in the place she feared most, the basement cells of Gestapo headquarters.

19

Eventually they came for her. The door to her cell was thrown open with a clang and two SS men grabbed hold of her and dragged her out. She would have gone willingly, but they force-marched her down the deserted hallway, into a room with a long wooden table. She was thrust down into a chair in front of it and then left alone.

Keep it together, Aubrey, she told herself. *You did nothing wrong, just tried to help a man*. Then she remembered her purse. It contained the compact with the false bottom that Hewitt Purnsley had given her. *So what?* she thought. The contact between herself and Agent Starlight had been aborted; he'd never handed over the important information. *Come to your senses, Aubrey. It's a spy's tool—they'll see that. It might be all they need to declare you an enemy agent.*

The door opened again. She did not turn to see who it was. This was all by design, of course: the terror of the unknown and the absolute authority of the state. When the man came around the side of the table, however, she gasped. She didn't know why she did; she had half-expected to see him. *Hauptsturmführer* Schmidt. Agent Starlight himself.

He had a file folder with him and dropped it on the table. There were other men with him, but they kept out of her peripheral vision. She heard something clunk behind her and the door was slammed shut. The sound hurt her ears.

The captain sat on the corner of the desk, crossed his legs and laboriously extracted a silver cigarette case. He lit a cigarette and handed it across to her.

Aubrey didn't smoke. She had started as most young people had, in school, and probably would have developed a habit, but she was soon bitten by an even bigger addiction: flying. The fuel and vapours and threat of explosion were very real around airplanes, so she had quickly dropped cigarettes. Most of the male pilots still smoked, and some of her fellow aviatrixes did as well, but she felt there was already enough risk built into her occupation. Why add to it?

But for this cigarette, even one offered by a Nazi, she was grateful. She accepted it and took a long drag. The brand was strong and foreign to her, but it helped calm her nerves just a tad. Not enough for her to cease being scared out of her wits, though.

"Miss Endeavours, you have been arrested and are being held for your safety by the Sicherheitsdienst des Reichsführers of the SS. Do you understand?"

"I'm an American citizen, a journalist. I just stopped to help someone who was injured, that's all. I don't think that gives the Gestapo the right to detain me."

Schmidt pointed to the SD tag on his sleeve. "We are not Gestapo; our mandate is to surveil all German citizens and aliens within the Reich's borders. The report here says you were causing unrest and acting illegally in the area of the entertainment district. That you led a charge of rabble-rousers against the authorities and threatened disorder within the Reich."

"Nonsense. I was having coffee with a friend. There was a riot, and we got swept up in it."

"This friend's name?"

"Richard Fuchs, a journalist with one of your papers. I met him at the air show just about the same time I first met you." Aubrey felt safe mentioning his name; they had done nothing wrong and Fuchs was a legitimate journalist. But then she remembered what Richard had said, that they had an arrest warrant out for him.

Aubrey carefully emphasized the word 'first' when she replied to Captain Schmidt. They'd had a second meeting, oh yes. She was convinced now that the man was indeed a spy for Hewitt Purnsley, that he wasn't merely trying to expose Aubrey as an enemy agent. If that had been his intention, he would have had her arrested a lot sooner.

Perhaps, when he saw her name on the arrest sheet from the riot, he had seen a chance to help her. This tough-guy act was just that: an act. Maybe they were just going to have a chat and then she'd be released. *Brother*, she thought, if and when that happened, she knew where she was headed: to the train station straight away.

"What did you discuss, you and this journalist?"

"We were just gabbing. You know."

"I don't know that expression."

"Shooting the shit, small talk."

"Is he your lover?"

"Gosh, no. What a question."

"When did you and this Fuchs decide to join in the unrest?"

"Look, we didn't join in. We left the café, went for a stroll. These men came around the corner with bats and charged us. We tried to get away from them. People were being beaten. This one man was on the ground bleeding, and I stopped to help him. He's a human being."

The captain smirked. "He was a Jew. He was an enemy of the state."

"Was?"

"He's dead, and good riddance. Another animal we don't have to pay to house for its own protection. We have reports here that you were involved in some radical rhetoric directed at our Führer at a café shortly before the riots began. Several people heard you and Richard Fuchs making demeaning remarks against him. That is a serious crime."

"I did no such thing."

"We have several witnesses; they have given statements."

"I want to speak to somebody from my embassy. I am an American, a neutral."

"A neutral? We're not at war with anybody, Miss Endeavours, and you are not under diplomatic protection that I am aware of."

Enough of this act, Schmidt. Aubrey fidgeted nervously. "Still, I want representation."

"Leave us," the captain barked at the two men behind her.

"Listen," she said quietly after the others had left. "That other night, at the count's mansion. I don't know how we can proceed."

"I don't know what you are talking about."

"Oh, really? When we were in the study. You approached me." She watched his face for any sign of a reaction. There was none. "Listen, just forget it. They can get the information out some other way. Just let me go, and we'll call it a day."

"Again, you are speaking in some strange language."

"I know who you are, who you're working for. I won't say anything, I promise. That is why you separated me from the others, isn't it? To help me. I appreciate it, really, I do, but all this talk of crimes and witnesses... You had me worried there for a second."

A fiery spark lit up the captain's eyes. He crushed his cigarette out under the heel of his black gleaming boot, then suddenly he kicked out at Aubrey, sending her flying off her chair. She went sprawling across the stone floor. He was on her fast, hauled her back up on her feet.

"Please," she said.

He punched her in the stomach, driving the wind out of her and sending her back to her knees. He rained blows down on her back, then picked her up again, his hands around her throat.

"No, you won't say anything at all," he hissed between clenched teeth. His face was scarlet with rage. His hands tightened, and Aubrey felt the air choke off as her lungs sucked desperately for air. She beat her fists against his arms, to no avail. Darkness shrouded her vision, and all she could think of was her father. She was going to die in this stinking room at the hands of this monster.

She didn't hear the sound of the door opening or the shouts of alarm, or see the arms of the man who grabbed the captain and pull him away. When his hands were free of her throat, she collapsed to the floor and tried to drag in air. Things went black and she passed out.

20

Aubrey awoke to the throbbing sound of the count's Mercedes. Moving, whirling lights sped past her eyes, which were just slits. She felt hot and cramped. When she tried to shift herself, waves of pain cascaded through her body, making the previous discomfort seem trivial.

She forced her eyes open and saw the thick red-carpet divider. Then she saw his feet out of the corner of her vision.

"You're awake."

"Yes," she managed to squeak out with tremendous difficulty.

"Do you want to sit up?"

"I do."

She felt his arms around her, and powerfully but slowly he helped ease her into an upright position. Her head spun and she had to close her eyes. Every part of her body ached, but her throat most of all. She put a hand to it; it was tender,

"That bastard did quite a number on you. I'm glad I got there when I did."

"You made him stop?"

"Yes, I made him. I would have killed him had his men not been there. You were nearly gone. I thought I'd lost you. I carried you unconscious out of that hell hole."

"Thanks."

"Do you want something to drink? Water perhaps?"

"Whiskey," she said, "and Aspirin if you have it."

"If you insist." He leaned forward and retrieved a crystal lowball glass and fixed her a whiskey. He even had ice. From a metal container in the bar, he extracted two pills. "You're in luck. I keep these here for when I've gone too hard the night before."

She swallowed the bitter pills and washed them down with the strong whiskey. It made her choke, and her throat hurt.

"How do I look?"

"Not your best, but you're alive."

"How did you know I was there?"

"I was informed. I think that maniac was stunned when I came bursting in. I knew I had to get you out of there quickly before he regained himself and stopped me."

"He was trying to kill me."

"It looked that way, yes. What did you say that provoked him?"

"Nothing. I don't remember."

But that was a lie: she did remember. She remembered the look on Agent Starlight's face when she'd brought up the notion of him being a spy for England. He'd probably taken personal charge of her incarceration so he could silence her. And there she was, with her chivalrous notions that he had just been trying to protect her. That animal. The only truly chivalrous man in Berlin, perhaps all of Germany, was sitting beside her now.

"Where are we going?"

"I'm getting you out of Berlin, taking you to my home in Bavaria."

"Why not France?"

"That would be inadvisable at present. Your name is still on a list of suspects. They may be waiting for you at the border with more men and more authority than I can overcome. No, we'll retreat south and I'll try and find a way out of this."

It was early morning when they finally arrived at the count's home in Berchtesgaden. Aubrey had finished her whiskey, and it had helped her sleep for most of the twelve-hour journey. The winding road up into the mountains afforded spectacular views of the Alps. There seemed to be an endless abundance of mountains. The spinning, twisting road with its steep drops over the edge made Aubrey feel like she was flying.

"What do you think?" the count said.

"My word, it's wonderful. How high up are we?"

"Eight thousand feet. My ancestors built a castle up here, nobody knows why. There were hardly any enemies that would climb this high to attack it."

The castle ruins loomed before them, massive mounds of toppled stone. There was only one complete wall with a solitary turret left standing.

"I told you the place needed some fixing up," Helmut joked.

The road took them through what would have been the main gate of the castle. There were huge stones on the ground on either side and the remnants of a staircase that followed the one remaining wall to the parapet.

"We can explore this later if you like, when you've eaten and rested."

"I slept almost the entire drive." She reached across the mohair seat and grasped his leather-gloved hand. He squeezed it back, hard. "Thank you for this."

"We haven't even gotten there yet."

"I know, but thank you."

They held hands as the car continued on past the castle ruins and climbed higher still. There was a building, certainly more modern than the castle ruins, but built on an ancient design. It was a lodge with peaked roofs, stucco sides and exposed timber beams.

The Mercedes came to a halt in front of the lodge and a man of sixty, maybe older, came out to greet them. He was wearing a green huntsman jacket and *kniebundlederhosen* and a worn alpine hat. He pulled a pipe from his mouth and squinted at the automobile. A haggard-looking hound reluctantly came after him and flopped to the ground at his feet.

Aubrey exited the car; she was stiff and sore from the long ride and the ordeal the day before. A hot bath was in order. The count introduced their greeter.

"This is my uncle Reinhardt. Reinhardt, this is a friend of mine, Aubrey Endeavours. He speaks English reluctantly. Don't you, Reinhardt?"

"Only in the presence of beautiful women." The man tried to bow deeply, and Aubrey heard his knees crack. His stick-thin legs looked strong, however, and his hands and face were brown from the alpine sun.

He was a very handsome man, and she saw a resemblance with the count: the twinkle in his eye, the square jaw, and the full, thick head of hair, though Reinhardt's had turned silver.

He swept up both of her hands in his exceptionally long but weathered fingers and squeezed them affectionately. Then he lifted one to his dry lips and kissed it. That and a wink from him, and she was smitten with this kindly old man.

"You'll keep your eyes off her, Reinhardt."

Reinhardt smiled. "I always knew you'd do the family proud. Welcome, Fraulein Endeavours. I will not promise to cease my attempts to steal you from this scoundrel." He grabbed her arm and, as if he instinctively knew she'd been through the wringer, he guided her gently up the steps of the Bavarian mansion.

Aubrey liked the kindly Reinhardt immediately and snuggled close to him as he led her through wide wooden doors adorned with metal, medieval studs and into a huge entrance hall.

He led her to a set of double doors at one end of the foyer, which opened into an expansive room with a stone hearth in the centre of it. A blazing fire was crackling away, and Aubrey could feel the oxygen swirling into the room from the open doors to feed the inferno. The hardwood floors were polished to a high gleam and the reflection of the flames danced across them. Above the fire was a polished copper flue that captured the smoke. On the wall were a dozen or more hunting trophies. Aubrey counted lions, African buffalo, American bison and a tiger. A part of her felt sympathy for the animals, but upon closer inspection she discovered they were old, very old. Perhaps the hunting tradition of the count's family had stopped long ago.

"It's wonderful, so... Teutonic."

"It's old and drafty," the count said. "I've a good mind to tear the entire thing down. I'm never here anyway."

"Don't you dare. The view alone is priceless. You can leave it for your children."

The count lowered his head and looked away, then back at her, and she saw the glint of tears in his eyes. He wiped them away and beckoned her farther into the lodge.

Aubrey chided herself for the careless remark. She hurried after him and was shown to the main bedroom. There was an expansive window that looked out on the mountain range. The side panes were open and cold mountain air filled the room. There was a vent on one wall. She ran her hand over it and felt the soothing heat of the fire. Suddenly, she realized she was exhausted. She sat down on the bed and winced. The scale and breathtaking beauty of the place had only temporarily taken away the pain Aubrey still felt from the attack.

The count came to her. "You're in pain—you should rest."

"Good idea. I did not sleep well in the car."

"I'll make sure you're left alone. I'll wake you later this afternoon for tea. We'll go for a walk, stretch our legs. This place has a way of making you forget the rest of the world exists."

"That's why you can't tear it down."

She flopped back on the bed and pulled him on top of her. He offered only token resistance.

"Aubrey, you have been through a lot. I want you to rest."

"Just one kiss."

He kissed her passionately and then pulled away and got to his feet. He pulled the warm, coarse blanket over her and went to close the windows, but she told him not to. Within minutes of his leaving, she drifted off.

She woke hours later to find the room in a pale blue darkness from the afternoon sun, which was sinking below the peaks of two distant mountains. The rays danced off the sheets of glacier ice flanking their sides. At first, she did not know where she was. When it finally came to her, she smiled. That smile faded as quickly as it had come when she remembered the events in Berlin. She shook her head and banished such thoughts.

The pain came back when she rose from the bed, but it was a dull ache now. She'd suffered far worse in the plane crash and had lived. She would live through this.

She found Uncle Reinhardt in the grand hall, stoking the fire. A scullery maid in a traditional uniform was carrying loaves of bread and curtsied to Aubrey despite her load.

"Fraulein. Did you sleep well?" Reinhardt asked.

"I did. Wonderful bed. How large is this place?"

"Fourteen rooms. Helmut's father had it built in 1909 after he gave up forever restoring the castle. Too much money, stone and mortar. Better to build with bricks and beams, *ja*?"

"There's this and the castle and..."

"And one hundred acres, most of it at a very steep angle."

Aubrey laughed and her torso hurt.

"You're in pain, Fraulein. What did you do?" he asked, concerned.

"Had a little accident. Where is the count?"

"Forget about those formalities and protocol here, Fraulein. It will go to his head. Helmut is out sorting the firewood. This fire is the only heat for the entire lodge. If we let it go out, we'll freeze. It gives a wonderful perspective on life, the balance we must all maintain. The heat is sent up through the main duct and reflected to the rooms. A chimney takes the smoke to the outside."

"I know—I felt the heat it puts out. Wonderful engineering."

Hands behind her back, she wandered over to the animal trophies. Their glass eyes stared down at her. "The count—Helmut—likes to hunt?"

"Those are not his. Those animals were walking the earth before you or he were born, I suspect. The hunting tradition has gone from our family, along with everything else. We used to own large tracts of land in Africa. Helmut was once, for a brief moment, one of the wealthiest dukes in the German empire. But at the end of the war, the Kaiser abdicated and our family was forced to renounce our titles and give up most of our lands. Germany's empire has shrunk, considerably."

"But Helmut's business—I got the impression it is very successful."

"Oh, he's made a success of it. His father invested in a small firm at the turn of the century. It has morphed into a conglomerate. Most of the manufacturing is done in the Sudetenland."

"Where's that? I've never heard of it."

"It's in that abominable creation they call Czechoslovakia, another edict from you Americans and the other victors in the last war. You really have stuck the knife into us. We barely made it through the twenties… So much turmoil. Now we're saved, at least for the time being, until the next war."

"I've heard that a lot." She didn't add from whom. Both her uncle in America and Hewitt had alluded to a coming conflict more than once in their brief time together. All the more reason to get the information on the new fighter plane without further delay and get out of Germany. If that was possible. She was safe here, for the time being.

"Don't you worry; the Führer has made more than one speech about reclaiming the Sudetenland. There are ethnic Germans there; they work at Helmut's factory. But he is worried. If they come under state control, there's nothing stopping that little Austrian from nationalizing them. And then, all this—*pffft*," he said.

"Reinhardt, that is quite enough."

Aubrey whirled at the sound of the count's voice, and then winced. Helmut was standing in the doorway. He wore a pair of tan pants that were tucked into brightly polished brown riding boots. He wore a heavy work coat, in contrast to Reinhardt's simple Bavarian lederhosen and white shirt. Maybe he was out of practice at being comfortable in the cold air.

"Helmut," Reinhardt scolded him playfully, "you shouldn't sneak up on an old man like that when he is talking treason. Are you going to turn me in to the authorities?"

"Not for the moment. I've come to collect Aubrey. I thought she could use that walk we talked about. There is a small café two miles down the path where we could have a light meal before dinner."

"Sounds delightful."

"I have a warm jacket for you."

"Lead the way."

The path was steep but, thankfully, strewn with broken pine boughs for traction. The sun's final rays flitted through the branches overhead. There was the roar of a waterfall somewhere deeper in the woods, and she could smell the oxygenated, misty air filtered by pine and earth surrounding her.

"We can go there tomorrow to see it," Helmut said, meaning the waterfall. "It's too late in the day, and besides, I'm hungry for my tea."

"What have you been doing all day?"

"Working on my automobile."

"Doesn't your driver take care of that?"

"I won't let him touch those beautiful twelve cylinders. Besides, he thinks it is beneath him. To get grease under those fingernails would be dishonourable. Sometimes I have a hard time distinguishing who the person with the title is. But I assure you, he never has that problem. He may not vocalize it, but I know his feelings on the subject."

Aubrey's laugh was genuine, and Helmut joined in.

They came out of the woods onto a granite ledge that ran for a mile in either direction. Before them lay the great expanse of the Bavarian Alps, huge beasts of rock and snow that scraped the top of the sky and made the clouds conform around them. Their peaks alternated between startling clarity and misty apparitions in the ever-moving blanket of white.

Aubrey had no words. She had not been able to take in the full majesty of the place from the confines of the Mercedes; during their drive, she had been preoccupied with the steep drop over the unguarded road and the terrible aches in her body. But now, the sheer size of the mountain range demanded her attention. She found she could not take her eyes from it.

On the ledge between the road and the drop-off was a château. There was a patio next to it, and as they descended the last hundred metres of the steep path, beer stein–laden waitresses in long skirts could be seen flitting amongst the tables. They found an empty spot at the far end of the patio next to the drop-off. There was no barrier.

"Don't people fall over the sides?" Audrey said, peering uneasily over the edge.

"Mountain people, such as myself, grow up with this environment. It's like any hostile place—the desert, the sea. You learn to conform to it, to live with it and respect it at all times. City dwellers are too scared to go near the edge. They creep along slowly in their cars. There are, of course, those half-breeds, the urban types who seek adventure, try their hand at mountaineering or high alpine skiing. They sometimes plunge to their deaths or get lost in the wilderness. There is a ski patrol that goes out to find them. I am an honorary member."

"Tell me about Reinhardt."

"That old codger? He is what we call ein *Bergmann*, a true mountain man. He was my father's favourite brother; there were six of them. All gone now, except for Reinhardt. He is the last link I have to a world, a life, that's gone as well. Gone forever."

"You mean after the war?"

"Yes. The war was terrible. I fought in it, flew fighter planes against the British Sopwiths and the French SPADs. I shot down twenty-three planes, then got shot down myself over enemy lines."

"You were captured?"

"I spent the last six months of the war in a prison camp. I was well treated, but I would rather have been killed."

"Don't say that, Helmut."

"It's true. To watch your country come to an end while you sit in isolation, to read about it, to hear it told to you by your captors while you await repatriation... Words cannot describe that type of anxiety."

She whispered now, conscious of the other customers. They'd turned their heads briefly when they'd heard the two newcomers speaking English, but now were back to eating and drinking their incredibly tall steins of foamy draft. Helmut insisted she try one, and now a waitress with an impossibly big bosom placed a heavy mug of beer in front of her. It was good, as ice-cold as the mountain slopes.

"Your country has certainly changed," she said. "For the better?"

"It's complicated. Has the Führer done things for us, brought us out of the doldrums of the Weimar Republic with all its sinful excesses and turmoil? *Ja*. I have to agree with that."

"Some would say freedoms, not excesses."

"Well, regardless of what word you use, he's brought stability to the country. He has ambition, and we're caught up in it. It is exhilarating, but..."

"But what?"

"He *is* a man with ambition. A plan. Have you read his book? No, I don't suppose you have. It's required reading here in Germany. Every house must have a copy. There are simple copies for the poor people and more elaborate gold-leaf versions for the likes of me."

"What's it called?"

"*Mein Kampf*— 'My Struggle,'" Helmut said. "It is a horrible book." He giggled and lowered his head, then looked around sheepishly. "Most people when they are alone will tell you that. If they are convinced you aren't an informer, that is."

"What's it about? What struggle?"

"It's the story of a man who sees his destiny laid out before him, and how the beatings and the hardships he had to take made that vision become clearer. And it lays out what he has in store for the future."

"War."

"Precisely. Tell me, how would one of your American presidents be received if he basically laid out in print a strategy and desire to conquer the entire world? How would he be received?"

"We're isolationists. We don't want to get involved in anybody else's war, especially Europe's. And we don't want to start one, either."

"Ah, yes. The Atlantic and Pacific Oceans are your buffers from such entanglements, I suppose. But your country has interests elsewhere. And those interests are growing. How long can you remain isolated?"

"Depends. If someone picks a fight with us, don't worry; we'll stand up."

"I know. We picked one, stupidly, and you can see the result."

Aubrey indicated her mug of beer. "My father always said 'Never discuss politics or religion while you're drinking.'"

"A sound policy. I would love to meet your father. He is still alive?"

"Yes." She felt a sudden pang of guilt; she had meant to write him, if only a postcard from Germany, a place he had helped defeat but had never visited. "He is alive and well." Again, more guilt; she remembered the revolver she'd snuck away from him. That reminded her: the hotel might become worried if she didn't show up for a while. They might clean out her room, put her things in storage, strip the bed and find the big heavy American-made pistol lying there.

"Helmut, my things are still at my hotel in Berlin."

"Yes, I know. Don't worry, I've informed them that you have left the city and that your things should remain where they are. The bill is covered by me."

She raised her eyebrows in surprise. "You have some pull in this country. Reinhardt said your title was in name only, but it doesn't sound like it."

"It's not that. But I do have pull. Let's just leave it at that."

"Okay. Great beer, by the way."

"It is. Let's have another."

As they were leaving, Aubrey spied a large brass telescope affixed to a post.

Helmut explained, "That's the Führer scope."

"What?"

"Come take a look—we might see him." Helmut took hold of the telescope and moved it back and forth slightly.

"Ahh, there he is. Come see for yourself. Our dear leader is taking his afternoon stroll."

Aubrey felt a rush of excitement. "Really?" She peered through the scope and saw two tiny figures moving along a path cut into the side of a mountain a mile away.

"That's Adolf Hitler, right there?"

"Yes. Walking with someone of great importance, no doubt. Two walks a day: one in the morning and one in the afternoon."

Aubrey pulled away from the scope. There was a line of three people waiting to have a look.

"Have you ever met him?" she asked as they started back towards the lodge.

"Yes, several times. You would like him, Aubrey. He is very charming. He would be most intrigued by your accomplishments."

Aubrey was flattered and excited by the notion. Then she remembered the snippets of his vitriolic speeches she'd read, translated, in the newspapers. The man was full of hate and venom, and, from what Helmut said, thoughts of war. No, she would not like to meet him or any of these modern-day strong men—Mussolini, Stalin, Franco. No, thanks. She'd take her good old FDR any day. Her father, a Republican through and through, might hate him, but she felt a special kinship with their polio-stricken president. He was a fighter. So was she.

21

Halfway to the lodge, the forest echoed with the warbling sounds of a trumpet.

"What is that?"

"Old Reinhardt, the archetypal mountain man blasting away on his alphorn. Traditional way for men to communicate with each other. He's going to bring the mountain down on him if he keeps that up. It's the supper call."

"He does that all the time?"

"No, my dear. He is just hamming it up, as James Cagney might say, for your benefit. We don't get many visitors up here any more, certainly not ones from America."

"I feel honoured. Don't get him to stop, please. I love the attention. He's sweet."

When they got back to the lodge, Aubrey went to freshen up in the bedroom. On the bed was laid out a ruby-red dress with black up-skirts and fringe around the shoulders. It was simply marvellous, and Aubrey was afraid to touch it. It was elegant yet sturdy, made for mountain weather. She held it up and pressed her face into the folds. There was a trace of perfume.

"Try it on," Helmut said from the doorway, startling her.

"Whose is this?"

"My wife's. I still have most of her clothes. Our staff have taken the more sensible items for their own daughters, but the formal wear is still here."

"Your wife?"

"She died. Several years ago. With our two children."

"Helmut, I'm sorry. I saw that look on your face when I mentioned children earlier. That was insensitive of me."

He shook his head. "It is in the past, and you couldn't have known. They died in an avalanche. I was away at the time. I almost missed the funeral. They are buried not far from here. Go ahead, try it on. Beautiful garments like that should adorn beautiful women."

"I shouldn't."

"I insist."

"Alright." She retired to the powder room, then came back out and stood in front of Helmut.

"Let's see it, please."

She twirled reluctantly for him, not that she was shy—she knew the significance of the moment for him and didn't want to seem garish or disrespectful.

"It is beautiful on you, as I knew it would be."

"It feels wonderful."

"Then you must have it. Take it back to America with you. You'll be quite a hit, even more than you already are."

"I won't protest—I'd love to."

There was the sound of a bell jingling from downstairs.

"That's Reinhardt, calling us to dinner. At least he's not using his alphorn indoors."

Reinhardt, with the aid of two women in the kitchen, had put on a feast for the ages.

"I am out of practice at eating like this, Uncle," Helmut said. "How do you pack all of this away?"

"This is a special occasion, and I work for a living."

"Uncle Reinhardt is the commander of the local ski patrol," Helmut said to Aubrey.

Intrigued, she turned to Reinhardt. "Have you had to do any rescues?"

"One last week, as a matter of fact. We were out for two days up into the southern mountains."

"We stopped at the café and Helmut showed me the Führer scope. I think we saw him."

"Lucky you," Reinhardt said, a hint of sarcasm in his voice. He upended the last of the Chianti into his glass and bellowed over his shoulder towards the kitchen.

"Helga, more wine, woman. You can't get good help anymore, not up here," he said to Aubrey.

Helga, whom Aubrey had only caught a glimpse of, came out of the kitchen with a bottle in her hands. She was a rotund woman in a long, swirling grey dress and tight-fitting blouse. She placed the second bottle of Chianti, already opened, in front of Reinhardt, and he filled his glass from it.

"Uncle," Helmut scolded him, and Reinhardt apologized and filled Aubrey's glass. She stopped him one inch from the brim. Helga busied herself with removing several dishes, once filled with schnitzel and sausage. She paused next to Reinhardt but addressed the count.

"Anything else, Your Grace?"

"No, Helga, that will be all."

Aubrey saw Reinhardt raise his hand and place it on Helga's rump in an affectionate gesture, and the woman retreated to the kitchen. She looked at Helmut and met his gaze with an amused grin; he'd seen it too.

After dinner they retired to the smoking room, and glasses of sherry were brought out. Reinhardt explained it was from his friend's vineyard in France.

"I think I strafed it in the war," Helmut joked.

"Very funny. His vineyard is far away from the front."

"Do you travel much, Reinhardt?" Aubrey asked.

"He never leaves his mountain," Helmut said. "His stories of friends in France with wineries is *bock mist*, German for bull..."

"Bahh," Reinhardt said, and he relit his pipe.

Helga popped her head into the smoking room. "Your Grace, we are done for the evening. If there is nothing else...?"

'Wait a minute, Helga," Reinhardt said, and leapt to his feet. He put an arm around the woman and ushered her out.

Aubrey let out a giggle.

"Not very subtle, is he?" Helmut said.

"How long has that been going on?"

"Thirty years."

"Why don't they marry?"

"More fun their way, I suppose. I know he's left her everything in his will, not that it amounts to much."

"Sad to think they've been playing games all these years, never to live together openly."

"They went on a trip to the Italian side of the Alps one time; it was supposed to be secret, but I found out about it. What about you? Any secret loves in your life?"

"There have been some. I've loved and lost."

"Like me?"

Aubrey thought for a moment of that day in Iowa. The crash, the smouldering wreck, and the burnt, twisted body of the man she had loved, however briefly. Loved with all her heart. They had never really gotten started, never took off, as he would have said. She would have been happy with him. She had had her own crash not long after that. Those months in the hospital recuperating, she had mourned his loss. And there was more than one occasion when she had reflected on her own brush with death. Had it been deliberate? Nonsense, she always told herself. The downdraft that had caught her was more powerful than any she had ever experienced. Any pilot would have been put in the dirt by that.

"No," she said to the count. "No, not like you."

"Here's hoping you never will. Tell me, that man I saw you with, the reporter from the Berliner morning paper—how do you know him?"

"We met just before I met you, at the entrance to the exhibition."

"I see. What do you know of him?"

"Not much. He's a journalist."

"I was told that you were seen with him, just as the riot broke out."

"We were having a coffee, a chat."

"They said he appeared to be quite drunk."

"Was he arrested as well?"

"No, I don't think so."

"Then how would they know?"

The count tilted his head, winked.

"Because I was being followed. Right."

"Or maybe he was?"

"Why?"

"He's a reporter who works for what was once a radical left newspaper. It should have in reality been shut down. He was one of their leading exponents of anti-Hitlerism."

"Is that a real word?"

"I'm not sure, but it fits. He could be classified as an enemy of the state. He may still be yet, if he doesn't learn a proper attitude."

"This doesn't sound like you."

"What do you mean by that?"

"I mean you're sounding more and more like that bastard who tried to kill me. Do you have one of those black uniforms in your closet?"

"No. I am a party member, of course, but I am not in the SS. They tried to offer me an honorary rank. I turned them down."

"Really? I'll bet that didn't go over well."

"They'll come back to me for sure. I can only resist for so long. It will cause offense eventually."

"So, one day you will be strutting around like that animal in Berlin?"

"Perhaps. But that is enough of this subject. I will not be berated for my views in my own home by an outsider, a foreigner, a…"

"Woman?"

The count stood up. He went over to a desk and spun a yellow-coloured globe around and around. "What do you really think of me, Aubrey Endeavours?"

"I think you're a fascinating man, certainly very handsome, caught up in a new wave of optimism. And ambition, like you said."

He spun the globe one final time, and it teetered on its stand but did not fall over. He came across the room to her and grasped her so hard she almost dropped her drink.

"I am developing feelings about you, ones I haven't had for a long time."

She could only gulp and stare up at him.

"I don't want you to go back home. Not even to Berlin. We can stay here. I know it's a fantasy, but I want it to be true, at least for tonight. And perhaps tomorrow."

"Fine. It is true, for tonight, then. Perhaps tomorrow."

22

Aubrey retired to the master bedroom alone. Helmut had explained that there were customs, appearances that must be maintained. Protocol. This had been his wife's domicile, after all, and the memory of her tragic death still permeated the place. He assured Aubrey that there would be a knock on her door later, when everyone else was asleep.

She found it all terribly romantic but admitted the large, comfortable bed was heaven to be in alone. She stared at the door for an hour, anticipating that knock, but eventually the wine and the fresh mountain air overcame her, and she fell into a deep sleep. She only roused when Helmut sat on the bed and put a hand on her shoulder. She rose to embrace him.

In the early morning hours before the sun came over the eastern mountains, Helmut slipped away. Aubrey was exhausted and filled with a warm glow of exhaustion and love. She had made a half-hearted attempted to keep him in her bed, but those damn appearances had to be maintained.

One of the servants knocked and came into Aubrey's room at seven. She had clothes folded over her arm, trousers of thick cotton and warm turtleneck sweaters. The girl spoke only German and from what Aubrey could gather, they were compliments of the count. The clothes were feminine in design despite their rugged functionality, and Aubrey surmised they were further remnants of the countess's wardrobe.

The maid gathered up the clothes Aubrey had had on since her coffee with Richard Fuchs and the awful encounter with the street thugs and took them away to be washed. Aubrey tried on the loaners; they were comfortable and worn in and appropriate for the climate. She went down to breakfast and found the servants preparing a table. There was singing coming from outside, and she went to investigate.

Reinhardt was sitting on the railing of the lodge's enormous front porch, singing to the songbirds perched here and there in the trees. They seemed content to sit there and listen to him; he must have them trained, she thought. But upon Aubrey's emergence onto the porch, they startled and flew away.

"Ahh, good morning, Fraulein. I trust you slept the sleep of queens and princesses last night?"

With a start, she realized Helmut was there as well, sitting in a wooden chair close in design to an Adirondack, reading a newspaper. He peered over the top of it at Aubrey's response.

"Yes. I hope my snoring didn't shake the timbers," Aubrey said.

The count smiled. He had not let her fall into too deep of a sleep for that to happen, of course. He snapped the papers. "Uncle, did you read here about the British fleet in the Baltic Sea? They're paying a call in to Poland and the little countries. With an aircraft carrier, no less. Very provocative."

"They want to tell us who still owns the oceans, any ocean, even ours," Reinhardt said.

"What shall we do today, gentlemen?" Aubrey asked. A maid appeared with a cup of steaming coffee for her.

"I thought we might take in some skiing," Helmut said.

"Wonderful! Downhill?"

"Of course. Are you experienced?"

"We took trips to Colorado when I was younger, with my mother. She always insisted we learn to ski. Part of her Quebec upbringing."

"I see you found the clothes I sent up."

Aubrey rubbed her arms and the warm sweater felt good against her skin.

"We'll have our breakfast, grab the gear and go," the count said, "Uncle Reinhardt, what do you say— those legs of yours still strong enough to handle the slopes?"

"I'll stay here, keep watch on things. You two go."

After a scrumptious, hearty breakfast of black sausage and eggs, the count and Aubrey headed out to the Mercedes. The chauffeur appeared from nowhere but the count waved him off.

"I'll take it, Wilbur; you have the time to yourself."

The driver did not speak; he simply nodded once and then turned, his nose stuck up at the same angle of the nearest mountain, and stalked off.

"He doesn't like me," Aubrey said.

"He doesn't like *me*, I'm afraid. Barely tolerates Uncle Reinhardt. I would sack him, but he's been with our family for decades. We've put his children through school."

"You think he'd show some gratitude."

"Old attitudes die hard. Let's go, my dear."

The two of them retrieved a large wooden contraption from a nearby shed and affixed it to the generous roof of the Mercedes.

"You going to let me drive this big beast someday?" she asked as they got underway.

"Not on your life, Fraulein, especially on these treacherous mountain roads."

"Fair enough. Besides, if I'm going to go flying over the edge, I'd prefer to have wings on either side of me."

"We never did take that flight."

"Yes, that is a pity. Can we still make that happen?"

"I'm afraid not, Aubrey. Tomorrow I must deposit you back at your hotel in Berlin. Something has come up."

So much for his dream of her never leaving the mountain, she mused. That ended pretty quickly. "But that was where the fighters were!" she protested. "Just a few minutes up in one, that's all I would need." She realized what she had said. "To fulfill a craving in me," she quickly added. "I haven't been in a plane in a long time."

"No dice, sweetheart, as your American gangsters would say. After I drop you at your hotel, I have urgent business in the capital."

"I thought your factory was in Czechoslovakia."

"I rarely spend any time there. All my work is spent stalking the halls of the Reich Chancellery and the offices of the Air Ministry. I have to constantly grease the outstretched palms if I'm going to sell the Luftwaffe any of my wares."

"I see."

"Besides, the 109s are stationed miles away, up north at an airfield in Kesselberg at the Luftwaffe proving ground."

"The exhibition is over, so I have no real reason to stay in Germany. My editors will want my story for their publications."

"I understand. We will have to make today and this evening something special, then."

Aubrey stared out at the twisting white roads, thin strips that wrapped around hills and the bases of mountains. Mountains so tall she could not see the peaks from within the confines of the mighty Mercedes. After driving for an hour, steadily climbing in altitude, they reached a chalet perched on the side of a mountain in the valley between two enormous peaks.

"This is it; we have arrived," the count said. "Mount Tidemoroff. I learned to ski here. My family owned this chalet for centuries."

"They lost this too in the revolution?"

"Afraid so, although I'm still given the run of the place. They treat my guests and me very well. Come and see," he joked.

They removed the skis from the roof, stacked them with some others and looked out over the ski hills. There was a chairlift hauling skiers slowly up to an unseen platform. Several more were zig-zagging down a fine blanket of snow. Aubrey worried about her skills; she had never really done the big slopes and hadn't skied since her mother died. That had been a long time ago.

"Helmut, my ski legs might be a little rusty. Can we do something smaller?"

"This is the smallest, least challenging hill. It's like riding a bicycle—don't worry. First, we'll get a hot drink and some schnapps and you'll relax."

The count was right. The château was cavernous and warm, and there were more people inside, sitting around a large fire drinking, than there were on the slopes.

"I thought we did this after skiing," Aubrey said.

"Nonsense. This is Germany. One always starts an adventure with a schnapps."

Several men greeted Helmut as he approached the bar. He spoke warmly with the staff and came back to her with two steaming mugs. The added schnaps did the trick; the coffee and booze warmed her and she felt giddy. Maybe she shouldn't be skiing right now, she thought. She needed her wits about her. It would do her no good to travel back to the States with her leg in a cast.

Helmut introduced her to some of his friends, and after a few blistering conversations in German, he and Aubrey finished their drinks and headed out. They had a chair all to themselves and held hands as it took them higher and higher. Aubrey gasped at the height and space of it all.

"What's the matter? You've flown a plane through the Rocky Mountains. What's a little chair?"

"I feel naked up here. This is too much of it."

"Don't worry; in a minute you'll be flying down the slope, and I'll bet you'll want to do it over and over again."

"If you say so."

They jumped off the lift and slid to the top of the hill. Aubrey ignored the view and concentrated on what she was doing. The count flew off, calling back over his shoulder for her to join him.

"Here goes nothing," Aubrey said, and launched herself forward. She took the first couple of hundred feet easily, moving in long lateral passages and turning in large arcs to keep her speed down. She used her poles to add drag. The count zipped ahead of her. There was a stretch of moguls to one side, and he steered towards them. After a few moments, Aubrey's old moves and confidence on the slopes started to come back. She would never catch him, but that was alright. She was admiring his form, and they would be together at the bottom.

She thought about what he had told her, how this was their last night. He'd made no mention of trying to persuade her to stay, or of coming to see her. He was a busy man, she knew. But the thought of it ending tomorrow, on some train platform or in the lobby of the hotel, seemed so cold and so wrong.

Then she chided herself again: You're in love with a German, Aubrey. Admit it. She felt butterflies in her stomach as she finally acknowledged it: she did love him. Then a new voice spoke in her head. You're in love with a Nazi, Aubrey, it said, and those butterflies became confused. Some settled down, and the fluttering of their wings dissipated. A few banged against her insides and jolted her out of her dreamlike state.

You're in love with a wonderful man, Aubrey. Rich and successful. He can give you anything in life you want. Like a career flying? That whole Nazi thing—we can work on that, she said to herself. With a laugh, she turned sharply left and pointed her skis straight down the slope, straight at the count, who was near the bottom. With a mighty push on her poles, she was off after him.

23

After their skiing, Aubrey and Helmut skipped the traditional drinks at the lodge. There had been something erotic about the whole adventure: sitting in the lift, hardly speaking, the sun warming their faces, holding hands... A few words at the top of the mountain and then down again. The count had been content to stay with this same hill, though the more challenging ones beckoned. Aubrey mentioned that she felt she was ready for something steeper but they ran out of time.

Instead of the warm confines of the chalet with Helmut's friends and more schnapps, they went to the car. After the skis were affixed to the roof and they had climbed in, their passion overwhelmed them and for ten minutes they embraced and kissed in full view of everyone coming and going from the chalet. When they finally separated, Aubrey straightened her clothes, embarrassed.

"I think we had a bit of an audience."

"We're still dressed. They probably want their money back."

Aubrey slapped him playfully on the arm with her gloves.

"Home, James," she commanded. "Home for supper."

"Are you hungry?"

"I am, but maybe we'll skip the meal?"

"I don't know, Fraulein; I have worked up quite an appetite."

"Yeah." She smirked. "Me too. Onward, good sir."

When they arrived back at Helmut's family lodge, Reinhardt came out to help with the skis and the roof rack. The sky had clouded over and there was a low-hanging blanket covering the surrounding peaks. It had grown decidedly chillier.

"I hope you have a fire going, Uncle," Helmut said as they made their way inside. Aubrey didn't realize how cold she was until she started stripping off her outer garments. One of the servant girls who worked for Reinhardt's mistress came hurrying out of the kitchen to help.

Drinks were poured and the two alpinists collapsed into the loungers surrounding the fire. Aubrey still stirred inside for Helmut, and he gave her a long, desirous look that only stoked the fires within her. But it would have to wait. It would be impolite to leave Reinhardt to go upstairs for a roll in the deep duvets of her bedroom. There would be plenty of time for that later.

"Aubrey, this arrived for you while you were out," Reinhardt said. It was a telegram with German markings on it.

"Telegram? Who knows I'm here?"

"I left word at your hotel, in case your editors had to get in touch with you."

She opened it. It was not from her editor. The note said *Where are you? Need to talk. Richard.*

"Who's it from? New York? Washington, DC?" Helmut asked.

"No, just Berlin."

"Really? Who would have telegrammed you here?"

"My friend Richard Fuchs, the journalist."

"Ahh. My competitor."

"Don't be silly. I hardly know him."

"You've known him as long as you've known me."

"But you and I have gotten to know each other quite well, I should think."

"Still, he pursues. I might have to shake him off."

"Scare him off, you mean. Don't be silly. Besides, you're abandoning me tomorrow in Berlin. Duty calls." She fluttered her eyelashes at him. She didn't want to admit it, but his jealously, fake or not, had annoyed her. She was trying to wink herself out of that feeling.

"Will you meet with him? You should."

"I don't know. We were together, that last day in Berlin, when I was arrested. Maybe it's not such a good idea." She remembered the arrest warrant Richard said had been issued for him. Chances were he'd already been apprehended, maybe as he was sending that telegram. Perhaps he hadn't even been the one who'd sent it.

"I see. Still, you can telegram him from here. Reinhardt can run it in to the post office, or we can drop it off tomorrow. It would get to him before you arrive in Berlin," Helmut said.

"Maybe. Let me think on it."

"Okay, then. Reinhardt! The lady and lord of the manor demand supper," Helmut bellowed.

Aubrey smiled but, truthfully, her annoyance had grown. No, don't do that, she cautioned herself. Don't let it spoil what could be your last evening together. She fanned herself with the telegram. The heat from Reinhardt's roaring blaze had rewarmed her and now was blasting her.

"I should go upstairs and change."

"Very well."

Reinhardt, sensing the impending departure of his female guest, tried his best to entertain Aubrey that evening. He had her in stitches at one point, doing an imitations of film stars and singers and dancing around on his spindly legs mimicking Humphrey Bogart or Lon Chaney.

She looked over at the count, and he too had a bemused look on his face. Then he stared down at the dinner table and fiddled with his napkin. Their eyes met; his seemed full of a coming sadness at what was to transpire tomorrow.

After dinner, Reinhardt permitted his mistress, Helga, to come and join them for a cognac by the fire. Aubrey could see she enjoyed being included as the evening wound down.

At last, Aubrey retired to her room. She had nothing to pack. The count had insisted that the clothes she'd worn here at the chalet go with her to Berlin. She permitted only the evening dress; it really was quite lovely. She insisted the warm clothes stay here, 'for when I come back,' she said. It was a test, a lob over the net to gauge the count's reaction. He smiled and nodded agreement, but did not comment.

Another stab of doubt and pain plunged into Aubrey's heart. Was this really going to be goodbye?

The count had provided her with a valise to take the dress. She packed that away, and then examined the clothes she hadn't worn since she'd arrived at the lodge. The few droplets of blood that had landed on her clothes during that horrific interrogation had been scrubbed clean. She would have worn them regardless, as a badge of honour.

Aubrey climbed into bed but could not sleep. Instead, she watched the door, tossing and turning in anticipation. Wanting the count to come in for one last night together, but not wanting it. *Let it end now.* It was well past midnight when she heard the light rapping on the door and the handle turned.

He came in, not full of passion but slowly. Almost hesitant. He sat on the edge of the bed. Made no move to come to her. Was this a test? She sat up.

"You look tired," he said. "You should get some rest; we have to get on the road early tomorrow. We really should have left tonight."

"Why didn't we? That would have been fine."

"Because I was delaying the inevitable, I guess. When will I see you again, Aubrey?"

"That is up to you, I think. You're a busy man, but a man of means. I'm just a poor journalist, a flyer without a plane. I have no visa here and no real story to follow anymore. Look, we both know where this is going. It was nice for a while, but you have your work, and so do I. I need to get back home. My father needs me."

"I see. We have tomorrow together, in the car." He started to rise.

"Is that it? Is that all?" Aubrey said. She wanted to lash out, jump into his arms.

He paused at the door. "Are you really going to let me leave?" he asked.

"Would you?"

He ran to her. They tumbled back onto the bed, threw the covers aside. The nightgown he'd loaned to her was practically torn off; his nails scratched her back. She did a fair bit of scratching too, clawing at his shirt. Their bodies were warm against each other, and he pushed her back into the pillows and was quickly inside of her.

When it was over the count lay next to her; both of them were wide awake.

"It doesn't have to be goodbye," he said. "I could arrange a tour of American factories; we're always looking for new markets to expand to."

"And I could dig up another story idea for the magazines. There's as much interest in aviation here as there is the States, maybe more so."

"The Führer has deemed it a priority that young people learn to fly."

"That doesn't surprise me." She hated the fact he'd spoken that word, that name, in this room after what they'd just done. It spoiled it. Don't let it spoil it, Aubrey. He has the right to say his master's name. Is he his master? No. If ever there someone who was his own man, a self-made man, it was Helmut.

They made love again as dawn broke. Neither of them slept, and it showed on Aubrey's face in the morning. Helmut had the car ready to go before seven, and one of the girls came down to prepare a small breakfast and some food for the journey.

Reinhardt was already downstairs, and Aubrey spied the enormous form of the head cook at the top of the stairs for a split second as she scuttled out of the old man's room.

"Aubrey, Fraulein, it was wonderful having you. You must come again," Reinhardt said.

Aubrey leaned in for a kiss and a hug and whispered in the kindly old man's ear. "And you must marry Helga." She pulled back from him, and he winked.

"How did you know? Am I getting too old to be a sly fox?"

"It's written all over your face. Just do it."

"*Ja, ma bin*. I will promise to give it some consideration. And you, youngster, when will I see you again?"

"I don't know, Uncle. It may be some time," Helmut said.

They bid their farewells to Reinhardt and his mountain, and the Mercedes sped them away.

24

The drive was long and quiet. The chauffeur must have known instinctively to get the journey over with as quickly as possible. There was a gap in the curtain and Aubrey could see the speedometer; it was buried. Cars blurred by as he overtook them, swerving in and out with ease, the coach rocking back and forth smoothly. They stopped at a small roadside stop for a quick meal that the girls had packed them of pickles and cold sausage and cheese.

They passed a truck that had run off the side of the road and was ablaze with fire, men scrambling around it, their hands on their heads in disbelief. That warranted only a passing grunt from Helmut as they roared past.

They came back down to earth only when they reached the outskirts of Berlin. It was late afternoon, maybe too late to arrange a train to France. She would talk to the hotel manager; maybe there was a midnight express she could catch.

The Mercedes pulled up in front of the Hotel Adlon. She half-expected that monster from the SS to be there, waiting there to pounce with a squad of his goons. If they'd found the gun, they would have good cause to arrest her. She might yet fall into that evil man's clutches again, she knew. Her fingers were crossed, hoping on that midnight express to France.

There were no SS troops waiting for her. The count escorted her into the hotel and went to the manager alone. He spoke quietly to him and then returned to her.

"It's all taken care of. They assure me your room is as exactly as you left it."

"I'll have to get them to print out a bill for the extra nights."

"It's all taken care of, Aubrey."

"No, Helmut."

He dismissed her with a wave of his hand. "My pleasure." He took her hands in his. She studied his face; there was the glint of a tear in his eye. Or was it just fatigue?

"I don't have much time," Helmut said.

"I understand," Aubrey said.

"When will you be leaving Berlin?"

"Tonight, if I can swing it."

"Will you be seeing your friend the journalist?"

That made her mad; he was still obsessing on this innocent connection she had to no more than a total stranger.

"Yes. I might ring him up, see how he made out," she said flippantly.

Helmut nodded his head and squeezed her hands. "This is goodbye."

"Not 'until we meet again'?"

"I don't know, Aubrey. Isn't it better this way? I look forward to reading your articles."

It was her turn to nod dismissively. "And I'll do what I can to follow your company. If you ever make that trip to the States, please look me up."

"I will, my sweet. I will." He hugged her, kissed her hard, once. Pulled her waist into him so her head bent back in a dramatic gesture. She was as limp as a rag doll. Then he turned and was gone. There was just the slight chirp of the tires as the large German car sped away.

The manager had watched with a smile as Aubrey's benefactor departed the scene. That smile fell into a straight-lined, blank stare as he saw Aubrey looking at him. Evidently, he did not think highly of the count's American floozy. All the more reason to depart the scene herself. She had no choice but to deal with him, though, if she wanted to get out of the city.

"Pardon me, can you please enquire about trains to the border?"

"Which border, Fraulein Endeavours?"

She almost replied, *Any border will do.* "France, please." *That bastion of democracy and freedoms. Get me there soonest, post-haste. If I have to sit in the baggage car, so be it. If I have to strap myself to the roof of the dining car and duck down for the tunnels, no problem. Let's make it happen.*

The hotel manager spoke to his assistant. "We're checking, Fraulein Endeavours."

The woman came back with a timetable and picked up a phone. A quick conversation with the train station and she whispered something to the manager.

"Fraulein Endeavours, you are in luck. There is a train tonight, at eleven pm, and there are seats available. Shall we make a reservation for you? You can purchase your ticket at Anhalter Bahnhof, the station."

"Yes, please do so. And thank you. Now I will retire to my room."

"Oh, Fraulein Endeavours, I've just been informed that you have a note here for you. My apologies—I got distracted with making your travel arrangements."

Aubrey took the note, assuming it was from Richard. She debated calling him while she rode the slow elevator up to her floor. Aubrey was reading the note, perplexed by its meaning, as she opened her bedroom door. She almost tripped over the broken chair lying on the floor.

Her jaw dropped as she was confronted with the state of her ransacked room. The note slid from her hand.

25

She quickly closed the door. The mattress was torn down the middle and the stuffing ripped out and spread everywhere. Her clothes were spilled on top of her bags, some of them lying in a heap on the floor. The magazine she'd left out with its corner pointed at the bedpost was ripped to shreds. What could they possibly have been looking for there? Even the picture of the room, which obviously belonged to the hotel, was askew. They'd left the light on in the small washroom, and she could see her toiletries lying on the tiled floor.

"My gosh," she said. Aubrey lifted the destroyed mattress and, to her relief, saw the large American-made .45 lying there in all its shiny, black, deadly beauty. Her only friend left in this country. A friend that could get her out of trouble as quickly as it could get her into it.

She let the mattress flop back down. There would be time for that later. She retrieved the note and read it again.

It was from Lydia, the girl she'd met days before.

Miss Endeavours, we need your help. Please go to the Bierkeller house on the Kurfurstendamm tonight. Order a gin fizz.

Aubrey sat on the decimated bed and thought about the note. Finally, she ripped it into tiny shreds and, despite the carnage around her, put the pieces in the wastebasket. She lifted the mattress again, hesitated, then pulled the pistol free. It fit nicely in her Louis Vuitton bag.

The Kurfurstendamm was blocks from her hotel, so she cabbed it. Her senses were on fire now. She looked out the back window, trying to discern if she was being followed. The maze of headlights crossing back and forth as cars changed lanes was dazzling. She gave it up as futile. If someone was back there, she'd never know it. She'd have to save what little surveillance skills she had until she was on foot.

The traffic backed up at the entrance to the Kurfurstendamm entertainment district, so she paid the driver and got out at an intersection. The street was busy with people, and she weaved her way through the crowd. She passed several rowdy bars, and a group of young men tried to corral her into one. She politely refused, but asked directions to the Bierkeller bar. She tried again in vain to spot a tail, but there were so many people; none of them stood out. She started memorizing parked cars' license plates; at least she could do that well enough.

The Bierkeller was quieter than the rest, and she took a seat on the small patio. She ordered a gin fizz as the note had suggested and saw the waiter talking with the bartender about how to make it. Then he came back with a menu and placed it on the table.

"I'm not hungry," she said, but the waiter was gone. She flipped it open. There was a small square of paper tucked inside. *Go out the back way.*

She passed the bartender, still struggling with the gin fizz, and headed to the hallway leading out of the back end of the bar. It gave her déjà vu goosebumps from her training session with Hewitt in France, but at least there would be no going out the bathroom window this time.

The rear door of the bar led into a courtyard that was well kept, with a square of lawn and a bird bath. Three-story buildings, the same height as the bar, surrounded the courtyard. She glanced up at the windows and fire escapes surrounding her. No one had seen her cross the grass, as far as she could tell. A man was pushing a broom at the far corner of the courtyard. She approached him. He didn't look at her.

"Keep moving," he said in heavily accented English.

There was a tight passageway leading out of the courtyard. She could see a dark sedan at the end of it. When she emerged from the passageway, the rear door of the car was flung open and she could see Lydia seated inside.

Aubrey checked left and right before getting in the car. Satisfied, she slid in and closed the door, and was thrown backwards as the car jerked away. The two women were silent for a block.

"Are we clear, Ernst?" Lydia asked the driver. Aubrey recognized him; he was the one who had tailed her after she'd inquired about Lydia.

"I believe so."

"Good. Thank you for coming on such short notice."

"You're lucky you caught me; I've been out of Berlin for the past couple of days. And I'm leaving tonight. My train to France leaves at eleven."

"There are other trains."

"I know, but I think I've overstayed my welcome in your country."

"Will you not hear us out?"

"Sure, for all the good it will do. But my bags are packed."

"My father is being released," she said abruptly.

"Oh? That's good news. I didn't think they did that."

"They do. There are so many people being put in camps that the state is scrambling to throw up new ones. Sometimes, with the right persuasion, or bribes, a person can be released. They released hundreds of prisoners in 'thirty-three, at Christmastime. A goodwill gesture—the last we'll see, I'm sure."

"Sounds like you have caught a bit of luck. I hope you and your father make out just fine."

"There is a problem. He is a frail old man, sickly. A year in that camp will diminish him even more. He has to be helped."

"And...?"

"We cannot show ourselves to the commandant of the camp. We will be arrested."

"And I won't?" Aubrey said, suddenly realizing what Lydia was asking.

"Doubtful."

"Not a lot of reassurance there. Why will you be arrested? Because you're Jews?"

"No, because we are political. The Gestapo has issued orders for our arrest. We are enemies of the state. You said when we first met that you wanted to help. Now we need you."

Aubrey sighed. "I'm leaving in two hours."

"If no one is there to assist my father, to sign for him, it is likely he will be incarcerated again."

"Where is he? Dachau?"

"No, much closer than that – Lichtenburg. It is where Berliners are sent."

"When is he being released?" *What are you doing, Aubrey?*

"First thing tomorrow morning. There is a train to France at noon. I'm sure you can be on it."

"Where am I taking Lazarus?"

"Not far. To his farm. We will provide you with an automobile. The process is quite simple. You show identification, sign for the prisoner, and he is released to you."

"They won't mind a foreigner signing for him?"

"I think they will just be glad to get rid of him."

"Very well."

Spontaneously, Lydia leaned forward and kissed Aubrey on the cheek. "Thank you, Aubrey. Thank you."

They had been driving in circles, but now they swung back towards Aubrey's hotel. They let her off on a darkened street three blocks from the Adlon. Aubrey made plans to meet them at that same spot tomorrow morning at seven. They would be at the prison by eight, and she could be back in the city on her way to the train station by eleven. She made a mental note to cancel her train ticket for tonight and move it to tomorrow afternoon. One more night in Berlin, she told herself.

She walked along the darkened side street in the direction of her hotel. A car was idling up ahead of her, its exhaust blooming out. The shops were closed, their doorways dark and gloomy. From one of them she heard a snort and as she passed, she saw a figure hunched up in the darkness. She looked back at the car, saw the plate now. Just as a hint of recognition came to her, along with the realization that she had seen it very recently, a hand shot out of the darkened doorway. The man pulled her violently into the little alcove and clamped another hand over her mouth before she could scream.

"Silence, Fraulein," he hissed. The door opened and the figure pulled her inside. He was strong. She lashed out with her foot and caught his kneecap, but he didn't budge.

"Aubrey, it's me," the man said. He removed his hand from her mouth and she stared at him, dazed. He flicked a lighter and brought it up to his face.

"Hewitt!" she exclaimed.

"Aubrey Endeavours," he said, smiling. "Look at you, alive and well."

Before she could stop herself, she grabbed Hewitt and hugged him. Then she slapped him hard on the chest.

"You scared the devil out of me. I thought I was done for. Thought those goons had their hands on me again."

"I heard about your time with the authorities, Aubrey. SD, was it? Nasty bunch. So..." He gave her a piercing look. "Why have you disobeyed your orders? You should have been back in France two days ago."

"It's complicated, Hewitt." Her eyes grew accustomed to the darkness and she saw they were in a furniture store. He must have picked the lock. "How did you know I was going to walk down this street?"

"I've been following you ever since you left your hotel. You looked like you were going out with a purpose."

"Seems like everyone is following me."

"I told you they would. I saw you get in that car."

"I didn't see you."

"I didn't want you to. What the devil is going on?"

"I went to the exhibition. I made contact with your Agent Starlight. Why didn't you tell me he was an officer in the SD?"

"I didn't know. I've never met him.

"But you told me—"

"That I didn't want you travelling into Germany with that information in your head. That was our prerogative, Aubrey. He's our asset. Starlight is an unknown to us, but his product is genuine."

"You used me to suss him out. What was so important he had to break cover? And to an amateur?"

"Did you get the package?"

"No. We were interrupted, by the Count von Villiez."

"The Count von Villiez?"

"Yes, Helmut. I was at his house here in Berlin, in Wannsee. He was having a reception for Hermann Goering."

"You met Goering? Oh dear. What was that like?"

"Yes, I was an honoured guest. He knew me, knew of my flying."

Hewitt stood back and raised his eyebrows. He was genuinely impressed.

"Anyway, I met Goering. Big deal. Big fatso with a twinkle in his eye. And after that, I made contact with your agent, Starlight. Great code name, by the way. Although I could think of a few better ones. He was about to hand me something when the count walked into the room. The exchange never happened. And the next time I saw this Starlight, he tried to kill me in the basement of Gestapo headquarters. Helmut saved me."

"Aubrey, I am truly sorry. I had no idea."

"I'm not sure I believe you."

"Where have you been the last two days?"

"With the count, at his ski lodge in Berchtesgaden. It's south of here, in the Alps."

"I know where it is."

"We saw Hitler."

"Come off it."

"No, seriously. Through a telescope. At least I think it was him. Just a little figure walking slowly along a mountain path. Anyway, I spent two nights with the count as his guest, and then he drove me back. Don't think I'll be seeing him again."

"We need to get you out of here, tonight."

"I've missed the eleven PM train."

"I have a car; we'll drive to the border."

"I can't."

"Why the devil not? You're in too deep here, running around with counts and Nazis."

"No, it's nothing like that." She paused, unsure how much to tell him. "I gave my word."

"This is ridiculous. You're coming with me." He grabbed her again and tugged her to the front door of the store. She pulled away.

"No way. I'm not going, not yet. There's something I have to do."

"What could it possibly be?"

"Not telling. I don't think you have a need to know."

"This is no time to get cute, Aubrey. You're in more danger than you realize."

"Oh, I realize it. I've been to hell and back, and it's not boiling hot. Quite the contrary, actually. It's damp and cold, and the devil wears a black uniform."

"That's not the only one he wears. Aubrey, there's something you don't know. This Count von Villiez is second in command of the Abwehr. He reports directly to Admiral Canaris."

"What's that?"

"The Abwehr? It's Germany's secret intelligence service. Aubrey, Count Helmut von Villiez is head of counter-intelligence. He is Hitler's number one spy catcher."

Aubrey swallowed hard. Thoughts of the past few days swarmed through her head.

"Is there a chance he is just manipulating you?" Hewitt asked.

"To what end?"

"What are you caught up in?"

"Lazarus is being released tomorrow."

"That German scientist you asked me about."

"I've been asked to go sign for him. His daughter can't. She'll be...."

"Arrested. Oh, Aubrey." He shook his head. "You're going to wind up back in the basement of Prinz-Albrecht-Strasse if you're not careful."

"Or worse."

He gave her a long look, and then appeared to have made up his mind. "I'll be at the Berlin Savoy for another night. Do what you have to do, and then let's get the hell out of here."

"I will. I promise."

26

Aubrey stifled a yawn as she manoeuvred the German automobile out into the countryside. She had not slept. Upon returning to her hotel, she had managed to get her train reservation moved to the late morning train. Then she had straightened the room as best she could. She'd even shoved the stuffing back into the mattress and covered over the large rip with the sheet and blankets. She'd considered sewing up the mattress with the kit she always carried, but she did not have enough thread. Besides, no matter what kind of repair job she did, the maid who changed the sheets after she vacated the room was going to see the damage. There was no hiding the brutality of the act; they had meant to terrorize her.

She carried her bags downstairs and had the concierge check them into the valet room, but she was adamant that she wanted to keep the hotel room until she left for the train at eleven. She told the morning manager that she would want to freshen up before her departure but in reality, she just didn't want any hassles about the room. A letter to the hotel could always be sent after she was safe and sound in the States. She would pay for the damages.

Ernst pulled up to the curb precisely at seven the next morning, into the exact spot where she'd been dropped off the night before. Hewitt Purnsley was nowhere in sight, but of course being invisible was his specialty.

She sat next to Ernst in the front seat, but they hardly spoke until he pulled to the side of a country road when they were well clear of Berlin. Lydia was there, flanked by two comrades, their hands menacingly stuffed into their pockets, their eyes scanning the surrounding countryside.

Lydia and Ernst went over the map to the Lichtenburg concentration camp. It was only five miles away and dead easy to find. Aubrey could manage it. They showed her the rendezvous spot, a farm that Lazarus owned. Aubrey repeated the instructions to Lydia to assure her she knew them by heart, and then Lydia took the map away. They would rendezvous with her at the farm, and then Ernst would drive her back to the city in time to meet her train. She highly doubted it; it was almost nine, and she still had to go to the prison, pick up Lazarus and drop him off. But she was already committed.

She got behind the wheel of the car and headed down the road. In a few minutes, there was a sign to Lichtenburg Castle, just as Lydia said there would be, and she made the turn. The castle now housed the camp; the stone buildings of the old fortification rose up above the landscape. Pockets of mist and fog hung low in the surrounding fields. Several army trucks passed her going in. She had to swerve into the ditch of the narrow road to let them pass. The backs of the trucks were covered in canvas tarps; she could not tell if they contained soldiers or more prisoners.

There was a checkpoint, manned by soldiers with submachine guns slung over their shoulders. The camp was encompassed by a tall fence topped with rows of barbed wire that stretched out in either direction.

She drove up to the checkpoint, where her identification was examined. She had prepared some German statements with Lydia and recited them reasonably well. The first guard, a corporal, was not interested in who she was or whom she was there to retrieve. She wondered why he'd even bothered checking her passport.

The next checkpoint was a half mile up the road. There was another fence, too; this one was taller, the barbed wire more menacing. The guards here were more agitated and watched her carefully as she parked the car in one of the spots provided. There was a group of army trucks and other vehicles nearby. She could hear dogs barking, and saw that several of the guards on the other side of the fence were patrolling with large German shepherds straining at leashes.

Aubrey approached the main hut; the eyes of a dozen uniformed men were on her. She tried to walk confidently, head held up, but the dourness of the place, the symbolism of absolute oppression, tugged at her confidence. Even though she wasn't a prisoner, the facility was having the desired effect. It was already breaking her spirit.

"Buck up, Endeavours," she muttered to herself as she entered the hut.

There were two men inside, clad in the black uniforms of the SS in contrast to the field grey of the

SS troopers. They were in mid-conversation and stopped when she approached, annoyed at the intrusion. Again, Aubrey said her spiel about how she was here to pick up Dr. Frick.

One of the SS men snickered at the word 'doctor,' while the other grabbed her passport from her.

"What is your connection to the prisoner?"

"He is a distant relative. His wife in the States wanted me to come and collect him, seeing as I was in town for the air exhibition at Adlershof Airfield. Personal guest of Count Helmut von Villiez." The officer handed her passport back.

"Sign here."

Aubrey signed and wrote her passport number down, next to the name Tomiel Lazarus Frick. They had dropped the "Dr." Of course they had; it meant nothing to them.

"You will go through the main gate here, and one of the guards will escort you," the officer said. "You will be searched in the presentation hut. The prisoner will be released to you, and you will leave immediately. You are not to speak to any other prisoners. You are not to hand anything to anyone or take anything. Is this understood?"

"I understand."

The SS man barked a command; his sharp voice shattered the air in the small hut. A sergeant came bursting into the room and came to attention.

"*Ja wohl*, mein Untersturmführer."

The officer explained to the sergeant what he was to do, and then motioned to Aubrey to follow him.

The main gate was slid open. The sound of dogs became louder and more intense; they sensed an intruder. The gate was slammed behind them, and another one that led into the camp itself was opened. She was led to a long wooden hut. Her purse was placed on a table and another soldier went through it. Thankfully, she'd left the .45 tucked under the driver's seat of the car. If they searched that while she was in here and found it, it would be curtains.

Then she was frisked, police style, and then ordered to sit while they brought the prisoner out. Eventually, a door at the far end of the presentation hut opened and through it stepped what Aubrey thought was a walking corpse. The man was positively grey. His unform was grey, his hair was a powdery grey, not white, and his skin was sallow and sunken and lacked elasticity. Lazarus removed the thin cap from his head, his eyes fixed on the floorboards. The soldier who'd searched Aubrey gave him a thorough going-over then shoved him towards her.

He was elderly, but Aubrey could not guess his age; this place had added years onto it. The shove almost sent the old man to the floor, but she could see a steely determination in his eyes. He was getting out of here on his own two feet. He was going to have that one small victory.

Aubrey said nothing. The sergeant showed the two of them through the gates again. Lazarus waited outside while Aubrey was shown back into the first hut, where she signed that she had received the prisoner. Then she and Lazarus walked to the car and climbed in.

The temptation to put the pedal to the floor was strong, but she resisted it. She drove away slowly, pulling over again as an army truck, now coming the other way, roared past.

When they were well away from the camp, Lazarus finally spoke. He spoke excellent English and started slowly at first, asking her name, who she was. Then he got around to asking how she was mixed up in the affair. She did not go into the details. Didn't explain that she had first heard of him from the mouth of a dying man in a field in Belgium.

Lazarus's words dried up, as if he had no more energy to speak. Instead, he leaned his head against the window and watched the countryside roll by. They drove in silence for forty-five minutes, Aubrey going over the directions to the farm in her head. If Lazarus recognized that she was taking him home, he did not reveal it. He made only one other sound, a deep, wracking cough, and she scrambled in her purse for a handkerchief. He had none of his own.

27

Aubrey brought the car to a stop in front of the farmhouse. It was obviously deserted; the windows were broken, the wooden steps were worn, and paint was peeling off the sides of the house. No one had lived here for a long time, perhaps since before the Great War. She wondered if she'd gotten lost. Lazarus certainly didn't seem to show any recognition.

"You know this place?"

He shook his head.

"I was told this farm was yours."

"I've never owned a farm. I'm a scientist. I grew up in Cologne. I live in Berlin."

Aubrey gripped the wheel, then reached under the seat and pulled out the pistol. Lazarus showed no signs of alarm; he just averted his eyes to the car's floor.

"Stay here." Aubrey got out of the car, the pistol by her side. Suddenly, she heard the cocking of weapons in the tall grass that surrounded the farmhouse. Lydia stepped from the shadow of the falling-down barn, a Sten gun slung around her neck.

"You wont need that," Lydia said.

"I brought Lazarus, your father. Funny, though, he doesn't even recognize his own farm. Place needs a bit of a clean-up, don't you think?"

Other members of Lydia's group now came out of the grass. They were armed with rifles, pistols, submachine guns. There were half a dozen of them, including Ernst, the driver who'd picked her up that morning. And there was one more person with them. Richard Fuchs.

28

"Richard?" Aubrey said. "What on earth are you doing here?"

"Aubrey, it's good to see you. I thought you were—"

"Dead?"

Another car—a Volkswagen, the people's car—pulled in behind the one loaned to Aubrey. A young man in a suit with no tie got out. He went to Lydia and spoke quietly to her, then took his place with his comrades. One of them handed him a pistol.

"What's the report?" Fuchs asked him.

"Luther says she wasn't followed."

They meant Hewitt, Aubrey realized. She certainly hadn't seen him. "You're part of all this?" she asked Richard.

"Our comrades and I want to thank you," Lydia said.

"Comrades?"

Two of them went and retrieved Lazarus from the car. He came with them quietly; he still looked defeated, broken. He gave not a shred of acknowledgement to his minders.

"You lied to me," Aubrey said. "He's not your father."

"No, he's not. My father is dead, stomped to death by the brownshirts. Most of us have had a relative killed by those Nazi thugs. We fought them in the streets in Munich, in Hanover, in Cologne and finally in Berlin. But he is somebody's father. We're members of the KPD, the communist party of Germany. Or what's left of it. Hitler has rounded most of us up, put us away in camps like Lichtenburg and Dachau."

"Like Lazarus here," Aubrey said. "So, if he isn't your father, then who is he? Is he even a scientist?"

"Yes, he is. A very intelligent and important one. His specialty is atomic physics. We're going to deliver our comrade, with Richard's help, to the Russians. They will have great use for him."

Aubrey had read in scientific and engineering journals about physicists like Enrico Fermi and the brilliant Albert Einstein, who had only just fled the Reich. She read those journals regularly, looking for articles on flying and aircraft development. The article about Einstein especially had caught her eye; the physics of it all were staggering. She would stick with airfoils, lift rates and fuel consumption ratios.

"Does he want to go to Russia?"

"He does," Lydia said.

"Why don't you let him answer?"

Lydia ignored her question. "Thank you, Miss Endeavours. Ernst will drive you back into Berlin."

There was the groan of a truck's engine from the hill that looked down on the dilapidated farm. All heads turned toward it, and then Lydia and her group froze. There was the squeal of brakes from the unseen vehicle. The group of communists started to spread out and were quickly enveloped by the overgrown grass and hay of the disused farm. Richard led Lazarus into the barn, while Lydia covered them with her submachine gun.

Aubrey saw the plane now: it was high up, and banking in a circle. It was a biplane, high enough that the engine could not be heard. It started to descend and the engine's sound drifted down to her.

"They did follow you," Lydia hissed.

"From the air, it looks like." Aubrey shielded her eyes.

"It must be in radio contact with them on the ground."

There were more sounds of approaching vehicles now, and they could see a cloud of dust rise over the side of the hill.

"We don't have much time," Lydia said, and she hurried into the barn after Richard and Lazarus.

Aubrey had to make a decision; in her mind she'd done nothing wrong. She had only gone to a camp and help drive a prisoner away, one who was being released anyway. She had no idea what this band of resistance fighters were up to.

Then again, she was colluding with anarchists, enemies of the state. Would the authorities make the distinction? They certainly hadn't in the cellars of the Gestapo headquarters, that was for sure. Aubrey ran after Lydia. Richard was helping Lazarus through the barn's dark interior.

"He's in no shape to run," Aubrey said.

"He'll have to, if he wants to live," Richard said.

When they emerged from the other side, the first shots rang out. They could see them now: a line of grey-uniformed troopers coming down the slope towards the farm, alternating between crouching and firing, covering their comrades as they descended. There was return fire from Lydia's comrades in the field.

Then an armoured car crested the hill. Its machine gun started up, and a steady thud of rounds started hitting the house and the barn. Lydia's comrades returned fire, checking the soldiers' advance. Not the armoured car, though. It came on slowly, the water-cooled Maxim gun clattering away. Rounds hit the barn, and splinters of wood flew everywhere. Then the gunner trained the weapon on the group as they moved farther into the field.

There were trees, the edge of a forest, at the other side, and they headed towards it. Aubrey and Richard helped Lazarus. He was wheezing heavily and missing every other step.

"He's never going to make it," Aubrey said.

"We can't stop. They'll kill him, as surely as they'll kill all of us."

"Are you a spy, Richard?"

"I serve the cause. The cause that's just." He nodded back at the soldiers. "I fight that. I oppose all tyranny."

"I'm not going to get into a political debate with you in the middle of a firefight, but I read the papers. I can spot a tyrant as well as the next gal."

"You're right. This is no time for an argument. Maybe we can have one over coffee some day."

"Agreed. Let's just get this man out of here."

They made it to the trees. The soldiers were at the farm now and taking up firing positions. The armoured car had stopped, and the machine gun was silent. Maybe they had a jam. The squad pursuing them moved past the farm and on towards them relentlessly.

"We can't go on like this," Lydia said. As they reached the shelter of the trees, the men took up positions and fired at them, slowly, conserving ammo. Lydia spat off a couple of three-round bursts from her submachine gun, but the enemy was well out of range.

"It's hopeless," Aubrey said. "We should give ourselves up."

Lydia laughed. "And go to that camp Lazarus was just in, if we made it that far? No, we make our stand here. For the revolution."

"There has to be a way out."

One of the men produced a classic German potato-masher stick grenade. He pulled the pin and chucked it as far as he could at the advancing soldiers. It exploded with a *whump*, throwing up a cloud of dirt, and the Nazis stopped and hugged the ground.

"That will give them pause," Lydia said. "We're better armed than they thought."

But how long of a pause? she wondered. Aubrey looked through the trees; she could see buildings on the other side. They looked industrial.

"There's something over there," she told the little group. "We should get to those buildings. Maybe we can disperse. Seize a vehicle, get out of here."

Lydia came to the same conclusion. "Viktor, Ernst, stay here and give us covering fire until we're clear of the trees. Then follow us."

The two men looked at Lydia but said nothing, just nodded. Aubrey saw the look in their eyes. Their nods of agreement were brave, but their eyes betrayed their fear.

"Let's go," Lydia said. Lazarus had collapsed on the ground and was gasping for air.

"I'll stay with him. You go," Aubrey said.

"Not acceptable. Bring him along."

"He can't go on; you're going to kill him."

"He's dead anyway," Lydia said.

Richard and Aubrey lifted the man up. Luckily, he had lost so much weight he was hardly any burden at all. Together, the group moved through the trees: Lydia with two of her men, and Richard and Aubrey carrying Lazarus. They didn't get to the edge of them before the firing started up again.

"We don't have much time," Lydia said.

"They'll be killed," Aubrey said, meaning the two left behind.

"They'll die for the revolution. We all will," Lydia said.

Aubrey had to admire the young woman's fortitude, determination. In another time, another place, they might be friends. She had seen these same qualities in the other flyers she knew.

They crossed the field to the buildings. There was a strong odour of meat coming from the place, and Aubrey recognized it for what it was: a slaughterhouse. "Great," she muttered.

In front of it were trucks with the snouts of pigs jutting out of slots cut in the sides of them. There were no workers, though; they must have fled at the sound of the approaching battle. The firing from the woods reached a crescendo, and Aubrey looked back once to see.

Lydia grabbed her. "They're gone. We have to move."

They entered the slaughterhouse complex. Aubrey took Lazarus to a bench and sat him down. Lydia and Richard Fuchs and the others went to a window and scanned the field they'd just crossed.

Lydia said, "They might be searching the woods. Maybe they didn't see us come this way. We can take one of those trucks."

There was suddenly the roar of an airplane's engine, and Aubrey saw the plane approaching again. Its guns started up and tongues of tracer fire came at them. The cab of one of the trucks exploded, sending everybody to the ground.

Aubrey recognized the plane; it was one of those Heinkels. If only she had a plane now, she would gladly take it and Lazarus and get out of here. If Lydia and Richard wanted to die for the revolution, let them. Lydia's group of renegades, as a futile gesture, fired up at the plane as it passed overhead. The sound of the engine dropped as the warplane disappeared out of sight.

There was firing again, and rounds started plinking off the metal siding of the abattoir. Aubrey heard animal moans and screams from inside. The truck that had exploded sent belches of thick black smoke into the air, marking their location. Aubrey belly-crawled to Richard, who was lying on top of Lazarus. He'd thrown him to the ground when the plane attacked.

"We have to get him out of here," Aubrey said.

Richard pushed himself up and looked at the scientist. His mouth was open, his eyes half shut. He checked his pulse.

"Was he hit?" Aubrey asked. She couldn't see any blood.

"No, but he's dead. Must have been his heart." He scrambled to his feet.

"We have to make a run for it," Aubrey told him. "They're going to be on top of us any second."

"Lydia!" Richard screamed across the sound of firing. "We have to go."

"You go if you want," she yelled back. "We're staying. We're going to take as many of the bastards with us we can."

"You'll all be killed," Aubrey cried helplessly, knowing it was falling on deaf ears.

"We all have a cause worth fighting for. Worth dying for," the young communist replied. "Maybe one day, you'll find yours. Go!"

"Come on, I'm getting you out of here before they encircle us," Richard said.

He grabbed Aubrey's arm, and they ran for the far end of the abattoir. There was a large pile of bones, and mangy dogs were chewing on the remains of a cow. Aubrey felt a wave of nausea wash over her. The dogs bared their teeth at her as she and Richard slipped on the bloody ground and staggered across the refuse pile. The firing behind them was growing in intensity, peppered with explosions from hand grenades as the German soldiers prepared for their final assault.

Outside, a dusty track led to another stand of trees. Her lungs and legs burning like fire, Aubrey poured everything she had left in the run to the tree line. She could see tall aluminum cylinders, silos of some kind. Aubrey cast one last look back at the slaughterhouse. She saw Lydia and one of her group reach the refuse pile. They were hit; she could see blotches of red blooming on Lydia's blouse. Lydia and her companion stopped and turned now, as the final assault came at them. There was a final burst from her submachine gun as the Nazis cut her down.

Aubrey let out a scream, and Richard held her head to his chest.

"We have to keep moving."

They reached the silos. There were no vehicles to steal, but Aubrey spotted two bicycles. "We can get away on those."

"Don't be ridiculous," Richard said.

"You have a better suggestion? We need to put some distance between us and them."

They hopped onto the bikes and pedalled furiously out of the compound. There were one or two stray shots at them, but they fell short. Richard and Aubrey paused only when they reached the top of the hill. The troopers had stopped their pursuit, waiting as the trucks approached. It was only a matter of minutes, Aubrey knew, before their pursuers were following once again.

"Come on—we have to try," she said.

They began pedalling again and flew down the other side of the hill. In the distance was a small village.

"We can get a car there," Richard said.

They glided into the centre of the town, trying to keep their expressions as casual as they could. The streets were deserted. Much like the slaughterhouse workers, the townsfolk must have heard the battle and locked themselves inside their homes. Their normal curiosity had been suppressed under the brutal Nazi regime.

There were only a few motorized vehicles, mostly tractors and a large truck filled with hay bales. Not exactly the discreet getaway car Aubrey had been hoping for.

She heard the roar of an engine overhead and looked up. The warplane was back. It flew over the town at a thousand feet, tilting its wings back and forth, but not in a friendly wave gesture. Aubrey knew what the pilot was doing: he was scanning the fields and roads for people fleeing. The trucks full of troops would be here any minute.

"They'll expect us to leave," she said to Richard. "Keep moving. We can hide here."

"No one here will help us, Aubrey. We're enemies of the state; they'll smell it on us. We'll find no refuge here."

Just then, a gleaming black car came roaring into the village. Aubrey recognized it immediately. It was the Count von Villiez's Mercedes. Her heart leapt at the sight. The rear door opened and the count stepped out.

"Helmut," she cried, and ran into his arms. They embraced.

"Aubrey, my dear."

"You have to help us. They're after us."

"Who is *us*, Aubrey?"

"My friend."

"Ahh, yes. The journalist." He looked over at Fuchs, who stood his ground, watching the two of them uneasily. "Who are you running from?" Helmut asked Aubrey.

"Soldiers. The SS," Aubrey said. "They attacked us. I got Lazarus out of prison, drove him to a farm and delivered him to his friends."

"Tsk, tsk," Helmut said, shaking his head. "Aubrey, why are you getting involved in matters that don't concern you?"

"There's no time to explain—they're going to kill us. You helped us once. Please help us again." She didn't pause to wonder how Helmut had just miraculously appeared in this small town.

"I helped *you*," Helmut agreed. "He, however, is another matter." He turned to Fuchs. "Are you going to tell her, or should I?"

"Tell me what?" Aubrey said.

"Richard Fuchs, alias, Richard Zorenko, alias Rudolf Zorenkosko." The count pulled a pistol from his jacket. "Go on. Tell her, comrade."

"He's a communist," Aubrey said. "I already know that."

"He's much more."

There were the sounds of trucks now. The pursuing troops were entering the village. It was only a matter of minutes before they were upon them.

"Tell her," the count repeated.

Richard shrugged. "You tell her. You're dying too."

"He's a spy, Aubrey, a Soviet spy. He reports to the Kremlin. We've been on to him for a while, but I never had the proof I needed to bring him in. When I heard he was working with the Rote Kapelle, the Red Orchestra, I knew it was only a matter of time before he would lead me to them. We could take care of them all in one stroke. And now, one part is done, Mr. Fuchs. Your friends are all dead. Now there's only you."

Aubrey pulled her pistol and put it to the count's head.

"Drop your gun or I'll shoot, Helmut, I swear."

"Aubrey, you fool." He swatted the gun away. She raised it again and pulled the trigger. *Click*.

"My men took the liberty of unloading it when they were in your room."

Aubrey stared at him. "It was you?"

"Yes. Convincing, wasn't it. I wanted you to be more agreeable to working with the Rote Kapelle. And it worked, just like it worked when I got you out of that dungeon. Do you think he would have killed you? That little rodent in the SD almost did. Good thing I had my timing right. Ahhh—speak of the devil himself. Here comes our friend."

The trucks came around the corner, and the count waved his arm at them. "Over here."

Richard saw his chance: he launched himself at the count, delivering a drop kick that sent the titled gentlemen sprawling across the hood of his Mercedes before dashing away. The chauffeur sprang out. He had a gun of his own and fired a shot at the fleeing Russian spy, but missed.

Aubrey stood her ground. A day ago, she would have gone to Helmut to help him. Now she loathed the sight of him. The SS troops jumped out of their trucks and surrounded her. They were shouting for her to drop her weapon, empty and useless though it was. They were just waiting for her to resist, she knew, for the chance they needed to gun her down. They must not know it's unloaded, she thought. Or maybe they didn't care.

She dropped the useless weapon on the dirt. Helmut's chauffeur scooped it up and handed it to Helmut, who had gotten slowly back to his feet. He put the gun inside his overcoat.

Then the soldiers were on her fast. They held her by the arms. Then all heads turned as Hauptsturmführer Schmidt appeared, wearing a smile that was half smugness, half fury. He still had the bloodlust of the recent battle at the slaughterhouse in him.

Helmut had recovered himself and spoke to the captain. "The one we want got away. He can't get far. Set up roadblocks on all exits out of here. Have the rest of your men do a house-to-house search, and call in for reinforcements."

"I won't be taking orders from you, Herr Colonel," Captain Schmidt said. "This is an SD operation. The Abwehr can stand back and watch if they like."

The count gave him a dark look. "Power struggles—that's all you people know, isn't it? Very well, run the show. I'm taking her back to Berlin." He inclined his head at Aubrey.

"No, I am taking her. She is in my custody," Captain Schmidt said.

"I don't want to fight about it. We can use my car; you can come along for the ride if you like."

The captain snapped a command at an adjutant standing next to him, and the soldiers started to spread out into the town.

"Make sure he does not escape, and I want him alive," the count called after them.

The chauffeur opened the back doors of the Mercedes.

"Aubrey, don't play silly games by trying to resist. You're in enough trouble as it is," Helmut said.

Aubrey knew it was true. She shrugged and got in the car. Schmidt and the count slid in on either side of her. Aubrey was forced to perch on the bar that jutted out from the back of the driver's seat and hold on to the red curtain for support.

"What are you going to do to me?"

Captain Schmidt answered her. "You're an enemy spy, an agent provocateur, sent here to disrupt the achievements of our glorious Reich. I ask you, what do you think should happen to you?"

Aubrey looked at the count and saw him roll his eyes at the pronouncement; he was trying to charm her again. Aubrey wondered if this was a case of good cop, bad cop. Clearly, they were both going to go to work on her, and it seemed the count was going to try the soft approach.

Helmut said, "Aubrey, why don't you fix us a drink. It's a long drive back to Berlin."

She relented, pulled out the crystal decanter and poured them both a drink. What the hell else was she going to do?

"Make one for yourself," the count said. "It will calm you down. I hate to agree with my colleague in the SD here, but he is correct: you will be kept at the convenience of the state."

"I'll want to call my embassy."

"You do not make demands here," Schmidt said. "You will only provide us with answers."

They were out of the village now, roaring along the country lane.

"Get your driver to stop up here," the SD officer barked.

"Why?" the count asked.

"There is a call box. I want to call for support. I've left all my men in the village; I want an escort. Just in case the Red Orchestra tries to free her."

"I thought you killed them all back there?"

"We took out one cell, but there are others—more than you can imagine. Although I'm not surprised the Abwehr has no idea what Germany is up against. Decadent, aristocratic fools. Driver, pull over here."

There was a shack just off the road. The count looked at the SS man suspiciously. The driver brought the big car to a stop and Schmidt got out, then reached back in and grabbed at Aubrey. "She must come too."

"Why?" Helmut said. "This is absurd.

"Simply speaking, mein Colonel, I don't trust you. And it will be my neck if she gets away."

"Mine too, or don't you know my boss, Admiral Canaris? He doesn't tolerate failure."

"The call box is on the other side of this building. I used it this morning to call in my men." Schmidt strode off, dragging Aubrey along.

"That'll be quite enough of that," the count said.

There was a voice from behind them. "I agree. That's far enough."

Aubrey recognized it: Hewitt Purnsley. He'd stepped out from some bushes on the other side of the road and had a gun pointed at the count.

"I'll take her, if that's okay."

Aubrey saw the bumper of a car poking out from the hedgerow farther down the road.

"I was hoping we'd meet, Herr Colonel," Purnsley said.

"She is working for you?"

"Indeed. On loan, you might say, from the Yanks. They won't take kindly to her being returned in anything but tip-top condition. Aubrey, come stand behind me. Move smartly."

She broke away from Schmidt and hurried over to Purnsley.

"Sorry it has to end like this, Helmut," Hewitt said.

"It's just a game, an endless game." The count shrugged. "There is always another round."

"I agree. Until next time, then."

"You're not free and clear yet." The count looked around at the surrounding countryside, and that mischievous smile that Aubrey had come to know, love and now loathe, appeared once more. "You're still in my country, Herr Purnsley."

Schmidt, who'd moved behind the count while the two intelligence men were talking, pointed his Luger at the count's head and pulled the trigger. It was the tiniest of pops, no louder than a Christmas popper, but the count went down like a sack of stones. The chauffeur's door opened. Hewitt spun and put two bullets into the chest of the emerging driver sending him slumping back into the vehicle.

Aubrey screamed.

"It's okay, Aubrey. It's over," Hewitt told her.

Schmidt holstered his weapon, then pulled out a piece of paper and handed it over to Hewitt.

"Thank you, Starlight," Hewitt said. "I'm also glad that you and I finally meet."

"You don't have long. You must go," Captain Schmidt said.

"Why'd you do that?" Hewitt said, motioning towards the dead count.

"I will call it in. I'm afraid I will have to tell them what happened—that you ambushed us, took her from me, killed the count and his driver. I was lucky to get away alive. To maintain my cover, I will have to order them after you. You have a head start of an hour, I'd say. You'll have to make your way across the frontier on foot. The border crossings will be watched, trains searched."

"I figured that."

"Poland is your best bet; I'll tell them you're likely headed to France."

"Thanks, Starlight. Aubrey, let's go."

She looked down at the fallen count, dashed a tear off her cheek. "Hold on." She went to him and crouched down.

"Aubrey, we don't have time."

"For this we do." She pulled her father's pistol from the count's jacket. "This doesn't belong to me; I need to return it." She reached in again and found the clip of bullets. She loaded the .45, cocked it and pointed it at Captain Schmidt.

The evil little man, in his evil little spit-and-polish uniform, did not flinch. "I believe she wants to kill me."

"Aubrey, no! He is a valuable agent."

"Perhaps another time, Fraulein. Good luck... to both of you." Schmidt started to drag the dead chauffeur out of his seat.

Hewitt said, "Come on, Aubrey. The clock is ticking."

29

"I followed you from your hotel this morning, saw you drive off alone. I even picked you up again when you left the camp with your passenger," Hewitt said to her as they drove off.

"Never spotted you."

"But then I lost you. Luckily that fighter plane let me know where you were. I thought for a moment that you'd been killed in the explosion, but then I spotted you with binoculars, running away with that Fuchs chap."

"Did you know he was a spy?"

"Suspected it. He is good, one of the best. I would have liked to have had a chat with him."

"He's probably dead by now. That bastard's men will rip him apart."

"And with good reason."

"What was it all for? What did Starlight give you that's so important?"

"You have no need to know."

"Damn it all, I almost got killed because of what you got me mixed up in."

"Listen, Aubrey, I didn't tell you to get hooked up with any Red Orchestra or a cell of communists. You did that all on your own. You should be in Paris right now, fully debriefed and on your way home."

Hewitt tightened his grip on the wheel. He pulled out the slip of paper and handed it to her. "I guess you were instrumental," he said.

She read the note. It was in German, written in ballpoint pen, hard to read. She recognized a few words; her written German even weaker than her spoken. She got the gist of it, though; it was an innocent-sounding note, a man writing to a woman about a romantic weekend spent in the Alps. Something she could easily have written herself if things hadn't turned out the way they did.

"It's a love letter," she said. "What's *liebessklave* mean?"

"You are really going to have to brush up on your German if you're going to be of any use to us."

"There you go again about the coming war."

"A future war is exactly what we're trying to prevent. With Starlight's help, we just might."

"With this love letter?"

"*Liebessklave*. Means love slave. The dot on the 'i' in that word is a microdot. It contains information about Hitler's imminent plans concerning France."

"Such as?"

Hewitt gripped the wheel tighter as he wrestled with going against his instincts, his training.

"He intends to reoccupy the Rhineland. It's a buffer between France and Germany, put in place after the Versailles treaty. There are French troops there now. If Hitler goes marching in with his stormtroopers, it might start a war."

"I see." She handed back the note. "He is a monster, your Agent Starlight."

"A necessary evil. He has the perfect cover. No one would suspect a fanatic of being a traitor. And that's all I'm going to say about him. We might share Starlight's product with your side eventually, but *we* run him."

"How are we going to get away?"

"I'm going to follow his suggestion: the Polish frontier. It's a hundred miles away. We can ditch the car and make it on foot if we have to."

They drove past a wooden sign on the roadside.

"I have a better suggestion," Aubrey said. "Take the next turnoff."

"What the blazes for?"

"Just do it."

Hewitt obeyed and saw what she meant him to see. There was another sign and an arrow marked 'fifteen kilometres.'

"You're out of your mind."

"I think we can pull it off, and it will be a lot quicker than driving or walking out of Germany."

They approached the gates of the Kesselberg air base, the one where the count had mentioned the flight trials of the Bf 109 were ongoing. There was a guarded perimeter, naturally. Two soldiers manned a white- and red-striped pole, raising it up to let cars and trucks enter. More soldiers stood lazily around, rifles slung over their shoulders.

"These are Luftwaffe personnel, aren't they?" Aubrey asked as they crept up on the perimeter.

"Yes. Their guns are still real; they fire real bullets."

"Just leave it to me."

The non-commissioned officer in charge approached Hewitt's open window. Aubrey leaned across the British spy. She spoke to the airman in a mixture of German and English and handed across a business card. The NCO read it, then went into the shack. He came back out and seemed reluctant to do so, but he ordered his men to lift the barrier. Hewitt waited for instructions from him and took the card back. The NCO instructed them where to park and which building to enter on the air base. Aubrey thanked him, and Hewitt drove on.

"What the devil does that card say?"

She handed it to him. There was writing on the back. Hewitt read it out loud. "'To whom it may concern: please afford this young lady all the courtesy and help she requires.'" He turned it over and his eyes went wide with astonishment. "My word, it's from…"

"Reichsmarschall Hermann Goering."

"The old boy got us past the front gate. Big deal."

"We'll see."

They were greeted at the administration building and shown inside. Aubrey, assisted by Hewitt's excellent German, told the clerk what they were there for. He in turn told a sergeant, who summoned a lieutenant and then a captain.

The Germans looked at each other. Aubrey produced her card one more time for all to see and read. She and Hewitt were allowed to wait there while the officers walked off to phone it in. Aubrey spied a handsome-looking flyer in a leather jacket and flight helmet walking from the flight line. She jumped up and ran to the door.

"Albert," she called.

The pilot stopped when he saw Aubrey, a puzzled look on his face as he struggled to remember her. She ran out of the building to him. Hewitt looked around; there was no one holding him back. He quickly followed after her.

"Albert, my friend," Aubrey said, and embraced him.

"Aubrey, is that you? What is this? How are you here?"

"We're meeting some VIPs; they're going to show us the Bf 109. We may even go up in one! Are there any trainers about? Two-seaters?"

"No, I am afraid not." He turned to Hewitt. "Who is this?"

"Albert, this is—"

"Carter Stowe," Hewitt answered, and extended his hand. "Air Attaché to the British embassy in Berlin. I'm escorting Miss Endeavours on her tour of the Luftwaffe."

"I see."

"Are you going up in a 109 now?"

"Sadly, no. I have been switched to larger aircraft – bombers. My poor showing in the air rally. You don't have a Luftwaffe escort?"

"Not yet. We were just waiting there for the Count Helmut von Villiez to arrive. He will be our escort."

"I see. This is a highly restricted area. I would hate for something to happen to you. Perhaps you should wait inside."

"Ahh, come on, Albert." Aubrey moved in closer and put an arm around his shoulder. She pulled the gun out of her jacket and stuck it into his stomach.

"Aubrey..." He winced.

She stuffed it right up under his diaphragm. That got his attention.

"What is the meaning of this?"

"The fighters—where are they?"

"This is an outrage."

"I don't want to have to blow you in half, but I will, Albert. I know you have a wife and child at home. You want to make it home to them today, don't you? I certainly want you to make it home today."

Hewitt shielded her from view as best he could. She noticed that he now had his pistol out as well, but held it inside his coat.

"The fighters are this way," Albert said.

"Let's go, nice and slow. No sudden movements, no alarms raised."

"I understand."

"Good. Big smile, please."

The German pilot led them to the last hangar in a row of eight. They walked past bombers and light aircraft, gliders even; all the hangars had Luftwaffe personnel in them, mechanics mostly. Aubrey hoped the last hangar had what she wanted, or they would be out of options.

It did: sitting on the tarmac in front of the hangar was a beautiful Bf 109. Its camouflage paint looked brand new, and the glass of the cockpit canopy reflected the sunlight. Aubrey checked her watch. It was four o'clock; there were only a few hours of daylight left.

"Is it fuelled up?" she asked Albert.

"I would suspect so," he said. "They are doing night trials this evening; right now, they're just waiting for the sun to go down. You don't intend to have me fly you out of here, do you? This is a one-seater."

"No, we'll just take it off your hands."

"You're going to steal it?"

"That's the plan. Hewitt, climb aboard and get behind the seat."

"What if there isn't enough room?"

"Suck it in."

Hewitt put his gun away and awkwardly climbed up the small, protruding two-step ladder attached to the side of the aircraft. When he was at the open canopy, he looked around. Then he pushed and shoved his way inside the cockpit.

"Now, I'm going up. I suspect you're going to run and start yelling. I'm going to keep my gun on you until we get that thing going, and then you can go sound the alarm."

"They won't let you get away with this."

"They won't have a choice."

She climbed the ladder. Hewitt's head was just visible through the back of the canopy, and he had his gun out, pointed down at the German flyer. Aubrey got into the cockpit, took a quick glance at the complex controls and found the starter. She turned on the fuel pump and heard a hydraulic whine. She pumped the flaps, set the magnetos and the pitch on the propellor. There was no time for a pre-flight check, but she was confident this plane would have been gone over by the best mechanics on the base.

Albert was backing up slowly, getting ready to turn and run. When the prop started spinning, that was his cue. Aubrey could have shot him in the back; the sound of the engine probably would have masked it. But she had been telling the truth about the German having a wife and baby at home. She remembered the pictures he'd shown her when they were in Warsaw together.

The propellor caught. Albert disappeared around the side of the large hangar, waving his arms.

"Damn it, the chocks," Aubrey said.

"Where are you going?"

"I forgot to kick out the wheel chocks. We're not going anywhere just yet."

She squeezed out of the cockpit, jumped to the ground, removed the wooden blocks wedged up against the two tires and threw them across the tarmac. Armed men came running around the corner where Albert had disappeared. They were taking their rifles from their shoulders, taking aim, their faces wearing looks of incredulous disbelief. They had apparently not believed their frantic comrade.

Aubrey dashed back up into the cockpit as the first shot rang out. She pushed the throttle and the plane jerked forward. A smile spread across Aubrey's face; this was a real thoroughbred, a greyhound, one fast cat.

Their speed across the tarmac increased quickly: twenty kilometres an hour, thirty, forty. She made a hard turn onto the main runway and pushed the throttle to the hilt. The plane responded instantly, and they were soon over one hundred kilometres an hour, roaring down the tarmac. She could feel the lift building under the wings.

"This thing can't wait to take off," she said to no one. Hewitt couldn't hear her unless she yelled. She pulled the canopy closed. Other soldiers, alerted by the firing or the unscheduled takeoff, were running to the tarmac. Some had weapons, but there was nothing they could do. The plane was going too fast to hit.

She pulled the stick back and the Bf 109 rose gracefully into the air. She found the wheel retractor. She'd never used one before, but gave it a try and heard the whine of the motors as the wheels of the thoroughbred tucked up under. Then the light went green.

The ride smoothed out after that. Moments later, Aubrey realized they were headed in the wrong direction, deeper into Germany.

"I don't think we can make Poland," she yelled back at Hewitt. He leaned forward as much as he could.

"Why not?"

"They're going to get their aircraft up, try and stop us. If we flew north, to Denmark or even Norway, that might throw them off."

"Can we make it?"

She checked the tanks. They were indeed full.

"Yes. What little information I did get on this plane from the exhibition was her range. We could fly all the way to France, but I think that would be pushing it, don't you? They would suspect that as well."

"I agree—try for Denmark."

Aubrey had no map, no heading, no radio operator, no homing beacon. All she had was an understanding of where she was starting and in what general direction freedom lay. She pointed the nose of the German fighter plane north.

For the next while, Aubrey had her hands full, learning the ins and outs of her new aircraft; she even nursed a humorous illusion that she would be allowed to keep it. She could certainly win air races in this beauty. The 109 was magnificently designed, and not just in terms of the flow of its fuselage and the seemingly effortless grace with which the wings rode through the air; the cockpit was laid out perfectly. It was designed to allow the pilot to maximize the abilities of the aircraft and focus on one thing: destroying the enemy.

There was a black cap on the top of the stick. She flipped it up. Underneath was a red button. She grinned; she'd never been in a fighter plane before, but it could be only one thing. She rested her thumb on it and then squeezed down gently.

The machine guns kicked into action, and the vibration rocketed through the entire plane. Bright green tracers zipped out of the front of the plane, through the propellor. There was a synchronization mechanism that prevented the blades of the prop from being shot off.

Aubrey let out a gleeful laugh.

"Aubrey!" Hewitt shouted at her.

"Sorry—just wanted to see what that felt like. Did it scare you?"

"No," he said defensively.

"How about this, then?" Aubrey pulled back on the stick and pushed it over to the side. The plane rose and did a quick barrel roll. "How about that?" she called back to him.

"Unless you want my breakfast spilled all over this cockpit, I suggest you refrain from doing that again."

She laughed again. "Very well. I promise you a smooth ride from now on."

"Plus, don't we need to conserve fuel?"

"Quite right," she said.

Aubrey fiddled with the controls—fuel flow, propellor pitch and acceleration settings—to get the plane at the perfect flying attitude. They were at three thousand feet right now, and already they were experiencing the chill. Neither of them was wearing a flight suit. When they reached the Balkan Sea, the expanse of water between northern Germany and the Scandinavian countries, they would get even colder. They would just have to endure.

The green pastures and rolling hills soon gave way to low, sweeping plains of hay fields and marshes as they approached the coast. The hum of the engine was hypnotizing. Aubrey was used to this sensation. She'd been on long flights before, knew how the hours ticked by slowly as the roll of the ground or water below lulled you into a dreamlike state.

Her reverie was shattered abruptly when the fighter planes sent to catch them opened fire. The lead plane came from behind, its machine guns firing a long, steady burst. Aubrey was ripped from complacency by the sound of bullets hitting her 109. She instinctively jerked the stick to the left and put the stolen fighter into a sharp turn. The stream of tracers shot past her. The pursuing aircraft then roared by, its nose pointed downwards, followed by another one. They were Heinkels, her old friends from that scary night not so long ago. They had come down on her from a higher altitude, and now they put their strut-mounted biplanes into a turn to try and come up on her tail.

It wasn't going to be like last time, though. Aubrey now had a far superior aircraft, and she was armed. She rubbed her thumb over the black Bakelite cap that prevented her from firing her guns, then flicked it open and rested her thumb on the red button.

Aubrey weaved and ducked, putting the 109 through its paces. There was a bank of cloud a thousand feet lower, and she dove for the cover. She needed time to think. Hewitt was silent, but she felt his hands gripping the corners of the small pilot seat from behind.

"Aubrey..." he said urgently a few moments later, through gritted teeth.

"Shut up. Let me think," she snapped.

The cloud enveloped them, and the canopy was suddenly awash in streams of water. She pulled back on the stick and cranked it over to the right in a slow, steady turn. A dark shape went past, a hundred feet off her wing, diving down. Then another one. Her pursuers had followed her into the low clouds. Aubrey pulled back on the stick some more to gain altitude. The engine started to strain and their speed decreased. She had come to Germany to find out the stall factor of Germany's newest fighter, among other things; now, it seemed, she was going to learn it firsthand.

Then they were out of the cloud, back into the fading daylight. It was already approaching dusk; the sun's setting rays filled the windscreen, blinding her. She quickly glanced around: there were no fighters, but more might be coming. She had to deal with these two, then get the hell out of there.

She didn't have to wait long: the two warplanes had guessed her manoeuvre, broken through the bottom of the cloud bank, seen that she was not there and then raced upwards to find her. She saw them emerge through the top of the clouds and turned to attack. She pointed the 109's nose at a spot in front of the lead Heinkel. It had a slower rate of climb, less manoeuverability. She was diving, increasing speed.

"Aubrey," Hewitt said again, an uncertain plea in his voice. He was looking over her shoulder, and although his view was restricted, he could see the enemy plane filling the windscreen in front of them.

"Aubrey, what are you doing?" Hewitt said, his voice cracking.

"Hold on," she said.

The lead plane was rising to her. It opened fire. The green tongues of tracer reached out for her, wavering, searching. Then they stopped. Perhaps the pilot had overheated his guns? Aubrey waited, closed the distance. At one hundred yards, she fired just as the plane coming at her reengaged its guns. She was quicker, more accurate. The rounds from her twin machine guns tore into the centre fuselage of the Heinkel. Sections of the cowling around its engine flew off, and there were flashes of mini-explosions as the rounds tore through the guts of the aircraft. Aubrey jammed the stick hard right and plunged down, past the dying plane, just as an explosion tore it to pieces.

She'd just killed a man, she realized. Perhaps a family man like Albert. But she had no time to grieve now, no time to ask for forgiveness. There was one more plane, and it would want to kill her now, more than ever.

She rocketed the stick back to the other side and then back again, over and over, swirling it around, until finally she put the plane back into level flight and a wide, sweeping turn.

"Do you see him?" Aubrey asked, her voice cracking with the strain, just like her passenger's had.

"Wait," Hewitt said. "There, at your ten o'clock. He's coming at us."

Aubrey saw him, turned in to meet him, but the other plane had position. He was better than the first pilot. He waited to get as close as possible before unleashing a torrent of phosphorous-backed lead on them.

Aubrey tried to shake him, turning this way and that. She was losing altitude. The throttle was pushed all the way forward; the mighty inverted engine in her sleek craft was screaming. Hewitt was shouting something; she had no time to take it in. The green fingers of death reached out, swaying to and fro, searching for the penetrable skin of the 109.

Aubrey pulled back on the stick, felt the blood rush out of her brain. By golly, this airplane was something else. Their speed slacked off as they rocketed straight up. Then she nudged the nose of the plane over into a loop.

There he was, her enemy: behind her, climbing as well, no longer firing long blasts at her. Perhaps he was running low on ammo. She felt Hewitt straining behind her, trying to keep himself jammed into the rear of the plane and not mashed against the now inverted framed canopy. There was no belt back there for him. Again, she dove, trying to get the angle on her prey. The 109 was faster than her enemy's craft, but the man behind the stick of that deadly bird had more combat experience.

Aubrey dove for the deck. The low hills and sparsely wooded planes rushed up at them. She could feel Hewitt slam into the back of her seat as they reached top speed. The stick was heavy. She had to use all her strength to get out of the dive. There they were again, the tracers: short bursts now. She wondered how many rounds of her own she had left.

Swooping in between the low hills, she saw the last of the rugged German countryside fall away. In the distance was a blue blanket of open water. Aubrey jerked hard right, driving back into Germany, then hard left. This time she kept the turn going, seeking her target. There he was: five hundred yards in front of her, in his own turn. Aubrey strained, mentally willing her plane to turn faster. The plane responded, and she knew she had him. She had reversed the situation and was now behind the enemy.

"Shoot him!" Hewitt screamed.

"No, not until I'm close." Aubrey closed the distance. The plane in front of her, as if sensing her approach, started a weaving dance of its own, but that only served to slack off its speed.

Aubrey's aircraft, superior in performance in every way, closed in for the kill. She was learning: she and the plane were now one. When she was a hundred feet behind the Heinkel 51, she opened up. Short bursts, just enough to let some tracer show the path of her fire. She saw it start to impact the target. Little bits of stressed aluminum skin flaked off and spun in the air, catching the fading sun.

Aubrey knew she had him. One final burst and she saw smoke billowing from the engine. Another burst and the plane exploded into a million pieces before her. Aubrey had no time to whoop, scream, yell or cry. She pulled back hard on the stick to avoid the flaming ball of wreckage she had just created, rolled over slightly and watched it fall back to earth, where it impacted in a farmer's field. She executed a quick S-turn to see if there were any other fighters out there. Thankfully there were none. She put the plane back on course. Hewitt reached over the seat and gabbed her shoulder. He didn't say anything, just squeezed, and then sank back into his makeshift seat. She had come through her baptism of fire and proven herself worthy.

She put the 109 into a slow, steady climb back up to three thousand feet. She would baby her dear airplane from here on in. A quick glance at the dials showed the heat of the engine was coming down. But, alarmingly, so was the level of fuel in the twin tanks. They were now below the halfway mark. There was nothing to do except hope it was enough to get to land, free land.

Germany dropped away, replaced by white-capped waves on blue steel–coloured water. The sun cast red streaks on the cumulus clouds to the west.

"We're not going to make it," Aubrey finally said.

"Don't say that. We must," Hewitt said.

"Look at the fuel. Maybe they nicked one of the tanks."

It was down to a quarter now, confirming her suspicions that the enemy fighters had in fact punctured at least one of them. So they'd made their kill after all, just a delayed one. Those two enemy pilots, brave as they were, would never know they had succeeded.

They flew on for another half hour. Aubrey slowed the plane back to a sluggish cruising speed of three hundred kilometres an hour. It didn't matter; the slower they flew, the longer it would take to reach land. The end result was still going to be the same. They were going to run out of fuel in the middle of the sea.

The fuel levels seemed to drop faster as they approached one-eighth of a tank. There was no point in trying to come up with a contingency plan. Even if she could do a belly landing, the plane would quickly sink, and without life preservers or a raft, she and Hewitt would too. If hypothermia didn't get them first.

Then Aubrey saw something amazing in the fading light: irregular shapes on the surface of the ocean, long lines with jutting ninety-degree angles. She was looking at the sleek forms of warships on the horizon.

"Hewitt, look."

"It's the fleet! My word—it just has to be," Hewitt said. "I read they were in the Baltic."

The fuel levels had dropped below one-eighth of a tank. Aubrey guessed they had a minute, maybe two, before the engine started to sputter and then stopped altogether.

"The big one in the middle, that must be the carrier," she said.

"Fly along side the fleet and put her down on the water. They'll put boats down to rescue us," Hewitt said.

"Nothin' doin'. I'm going to land on that sucker. It looks big enough."

"Aubrey, you're insane! You can't do it."

Aubrey felt the first indication the engine was running out of fuel: a misstep in its firing, then another. They started to come regularly and faster. The whole airplane started to shudder.

"That's it. She's dry," Aubrey said just as she lined up behind the carrier. They were flying into the wind now when the engine stopped altogether. There was a wispy, eerie silence. She felt the drag of the wind, and her speed started to slow. Aubrey had glided a plane to a landing before, in Texas. That time, she hadn't run out of fuel, though; it had been just a mechanical failure of the fuel pump. But that was Texas, great big Texas, with miles and miles of flat land. Big, beautiful wide roads and farm tracks, there for the picking. This was a piece of moving, heaving steel and wood, a football field long.

Aubrey could see people scrambling on the wooden flight deck as she came in. She'd seen newsreels of aircraft carrier operation before, knew about the various arresting devices that carrier-borne aircraft were equipped with. She knew her Bf 109 had none of that. It was not meant to land on a floating airport. This was going to be a first, one for the record books.

"Are you going to put the landing gear down?" Hewitt asked. He had no need to scream now that the motor was out of fuel.

"No can do. That requires the engine."

"Isn't there a hand crank or a button? Maybe it's wired to a separate battery, just for a contingency like this."

"No time to figure it out. We're going in. Hold on, Hewitt, here we go." She dipped the nose down, picking up a bit of speed she'd lost. The plane glided almost as nicely as it flew. The carrier got larger and larger in the cockpit canopy.

"Just keep your thumb off the machine guns," Hewitt said.

Aubrey laughed. She made sure the safety cap was over the red firing button as she pulled the nose up at the last second. The edge of the deck swung under the plane. There was a row of Swordfish torpedo planes to her right. With no way to lower the undercarriage, a belly landing was her only option. This saddened her; a belly landing was going to damage her nice plane. The prop would be ruined. But at least it wouldn't wind up at the bottom of the sea.

The plane hit, and there was a sickening skid of aluminum on the wooden flight deck. There was a crunch and grind as the plane ran over the arresting cable. She hoped it might catch the fixed rear wheel, but it did not. They slid on, past the warplanes, past the looming control tower.

Aubrey held up her hand; there was no point trying to control the plane now. Hewitt reached forward and grabbed it. They were slowing, but not enough. The bow of the aircraft carrier was steadily approaching. Finally, the stolen fighter came to a stop just as the damaged propellor slid over the edge of the ship's bow.

"Wow," Aubrey said.

Hewitt squeezed her hand harder. "We made it, old girl. You did it."

"Yes, I did, didn't I?"

Surrounded on the deck by sailors and a few Royal Marines, suitably armed, Aubrey let Hewitt do the talking. He quickly explained their predicament, without going into the sensitive details. The men of *HMS Eagle* swarmed over the German fighter until some senior officers came and sent everybody back to their stations. A cable was attached to the rear of the 109 to drag it back from the edge. Aubrey gave the aircraft a last affectionate pat as she and Hewitt were led into the ship.

They were escorted into the wardroom, where they were given tea and biscuits. They went over the whole ordeal one more time for the captain and his XO. The two seasoned salts of His Majesty's Royal Navy looked at each other incredulously. Then they clapped Hewitt on the shoulder and said, "Well done."

"It was all thanks to Miss Endeavours, sir. If she wasn't probably the world's greatest flyer, and the bravest woman I've ever met, right now Herr Hitler would have me on a rack."

The captain remarked on what an incredible feat the landing had been, and he shook Aubrey's hand. Then he took a small notebook and pen out of his breast pocket.

"I've never done this before, but Miss Endeavours, may I have your autograph?"

30

Aubrey stepped down off the ocean liner's gangplank and resisted the urge to kneel down and kiss the dirty asphalt dock. She was just thankful to be home. The crowds of people coming off the ship eventually cleared, and Aubrey had just got in the line to the New York Port Authority customs office when she heard a whistle. It was her uncle Arthur, standing next to a sleek black Buick. He waved her over. Her belongings had been left behind in Germany, no doubt the property of the Gestapo by now. But she had her father's handgun tucked safely inside her new Louis Vuitton bag. Hewitt had taken her on a shopping spree in Paris, courtesy of British Intelligence. She'd arrived back in New York, decked out in some of the finest Parisian fashions and carrying some sleek new luggage.

"Mr. Walton."

Arthur smiled. "Come on, Aubrey. Let's get you home."

"What about customs?"

"It's all taken care of."

Aubrey shrugged and got into the car.

They were far away from the dock before he spoke again. "So how was Europe?"

"Europe was… interesting."

"I'll bet. I read Purnsley's report but we'll need to debrief you. Seems you had quite the little adventure."

"I'll say."

"Good to be home, though?"

"It is."

"Bet you're anxious to see your father."

"Oh, yes."

"Just one question."

"Uh-huh."

"Are you done working for me, Aubrey? Or do you want another taste of this life?"

"Well, Mr. Walton…" Aubrey said. She sucked in a deep breath. Her mind went back to the soaring Alps, their height matched only by the love, however brief, she'd felt for Helmut. Then she thought of him lying dead by the side of the road, and the feelings of anger and sadness she'd felt. But most of all, she thought of a brave gentleman from British Intelligence and how she would very much like to see him again.

"…you'd better believe I do."

"I'm glad, Aubrey. Now let's get you home."

The End

Hope you enjoyed this book, please leave a star rating or review.

Printed in Great Britain
by Amazon